David Gainer, boy, you've proven yourself worthy more times than I can count. Thanks for what you've done. To the bookstores that push ***Stick & Move I, II, and III***: thanks for putting my name out there.

Richard Jeanty: thanks for everything. I've learned a lot of valuable things from you and I hope that our future endeavors will prove worthy.

To the African-American bookstores: thank you for putting my work out and getting me the recognition I very much need. I'll be sure to give back to the community.

And lastly, again, I would like to thank each and every reader who continues to support my novels. I promise to give you more exciting reads that will have you questioning things about yourself.

I'm signing off!

PROLOGUE

"Damnit, man!" Shukre cursed through clenched teeth. He was hiding underneath a table in the center of the room, crouched in the fetal position, trying to ward off fierce blows. Each time the stick would connect, a bone would crack, break, or shatter upon impact.

Earlier that day, while taking part in a shared routine by most of the inmates housed in his pod - pull-ups, push-ups and dips - he was called to the front desk where an officer was waiting. The wrinkled expression on his face told of his annoyance as he demanded of the c.o., "What the fuck y'all want with me now?" Wiping sweat that was dripping down his forehead, Shukre didn't resist when the officer placed the cuffs around his wrist and escorted him down a long hallway. Entering through a door that was used as a conference room for visiting attorneys, Shukre was shocked to find two men in suits standing with their backs to him. They were busy sifting through a thick file, presumably his.

"Take a seat, Mr. Herring," the shorter of the two said, "Or should I call you Shukre?" Immediately, Shukre's trouble antenna went up; he knew something was about to go down. For seconds, he stared at the two figures, still not sure of where he knew them from. Shukre knew the moment his name was mentioned some shit was about to jump off. Turning to the officer who escorted him to the room, Shukre said, "Look, I didn't call for any lawyers, so I'd appreciate it if you took me back to my cell."

The guard eyed the two men. "That'll be all," the taller gentleman said. "We'll take it from here."

The loud thud of the door closing caused Shukre to jump. His instincts warned him something was about to happen as he watched the short man retrieve a solid, steel baton from his side. The man tapped the stick lightly against the palm of his hand. Eyeing Shukre, he began to talk. "I'm only going to ask you these questions once. Dalvin Fleming - where can I find him?"

The man's tone conveyed the seriousness of the situation as he implied Shukre knew this Dalvin Fleming but he wasn't about to tell them anything. The men had done this type of work many times before; it was their job to search for and recover people and information. One thing they didn't like was to be deceived. Before giving Shukre a chance to answer, the taller man spoke. "Mr. Herring, if you lie to us we'll know and believe me, the pain we deliver won't be bearable. Let's make this as simple and easy as possible." Shukre pondered this, realizing the men had the upper-hand. He was still in cuffs and was quite sure he couldn't take both of the men at once. Without hesitating he said, "Honestly, I don't know where to find him. I mean, I've been locked up for the past three mo--."

The force of the steel rod slashing through the air left a whooshing sound in Shukre's ears. With no time to react, he watched the baton crack down on his hand.

He cried out in pain, screaming, "What the fuck you do that for?" He bent over in tears holding his limp, throbbing hand that was already beginning to swell. Sweat beads began to form on his forehead. As he leaned over to try and alleviate the discomfort, he trembled from fear.

"Second question."

Though Shukre could hear the man mumble something, it was if he was stuck inside a can two hundred fifty feet below the ocean; everything he was hearing seemed distorted. In his mind, he wondered who these men really were. They didn't bother to flash their credentials, or tell him who they worked for. One thing was certain as he whimpered from the pain in his wrist, (which now was being constricted by the cuffs) whoever they were getting their information was on point.

"The girl, Yasmina, where is she?"

Shukre couldn't answer the question fast enough before the baton smashed his other hand. He let out another piercing scream. "Look, muthafucka!" He gritted his teeth trying to fight the relentless discomfort. "I don't know why y'all are questioning me about this shit. I had nothing to do with any fucking prison break."

As soon as the words left Shukre's mouth the men eyed each other. "He knows something," the shorter man yelled. "I never mentioned anything about a prison break."

For what seemed to Shukre like hours, but were in fact only minutes, he suffered a fierce and painful beating. His nose, both legs and arms, fingers, the sockets of his eyes, even his toes were broken or ruptured. Despite the vicious assault, Shukre fought with all the strength his weak and bruised body could muster. Through it he uttered, "No matter how much you beat me, I'm still not telling you shit!" Though full of conviction, his words fell on deaf ears; these two men had witnessed this type of arrogance before, and they were convinced that by the end of the meeting, they would get the information they needed.

The smaller man laughed. "Mr. Herring you're strong but foolish, and it amazes me how some people choose to make the least wise decisions at the most important times." Shukre coughed, grimacing in agony. Through wheezing and labored breathing he mumbled, "I'll die before I turn on my friends."

The comment caused both men to chuckle. "Killing you will be the easy part," the taller of the two said. He dangled a photo in front of Shukre. "But having your family watch each other die a slow and painful death will be even more fun." The thought alone caused Shukre to shudder, but it was the look in the man's eyes that shook him to the core and forced a tear down Shukre's cheek. The realization that his life would end soon, coupled with the fact that his body was numb sent him to the place that still held a trace of sensation - his heart. Curling his lips, he smiled at fond memories he'd shared with both his family and Dalvin. He also knew that giving these people what they wanted meant death on a larger scale. He shook his head from side to side. "For you to already have that picture of my family means they're already dead." Shukre struggled to swallow the huge lump in his throat. Fighting back tears he cursed, "When you reach hell, I'll be waiting for ya', you bitch ass muthafucka!"

He died seconds later as the taller man choked him with his bare hands.

CHAPTER ONE

PRESENT DAY:

FRIBOURG, SWITZERLAND
6:30 A.M

"I apologize, Ms., but we must hurry," the brotha said, grabbing Yasmina's arm.

Yasmina fought to steady herself as they walked down the steep flight of steps leading from the plane. It was obvious just how much of a hurry the man was in when he raced toward a small European vehicle, tossed her in the backseat, tapped the driver on the shoulder, then shouted, "DRIVE!"

The car squealed as it kicked back rocks, gravel, all sorts of debris and sped away from the tarmac. Yasmina looked at the small strip of pavement being used as a road, and a landing strip for Lear jets, Cessnas, and other planes and had no idea where she was. They drove a few miles down the highway and the once-sparse traffic grew heavier. Signs read: *Boltigen .4 kilometers. Gruyeres 26 kilometers. Geneve 130 kilometers.* Yasmina tried to sound out the words, but she couldn't. She realized that she could only be in one place - Europe.

Yasmina wasn't comfortable being in the presence of a complete stranger. She glanced in the man's direction then quickly jerked her head back into its previous position. He was staring at her. Panic and fear settled over Yasmina; the thought of being stuck in a car in a foreign country with this strange man caused her to stare right back at him. She was surprised to realize the man wasn't paying the least bit of attention to her. For moments her eyes ran up and down his frame, looking at his attire: a dark-brimmed hat slightly covered his face, dark shades hid his eyes, a three-quarter-length leather jacket was wrapped around his waist and a pair of black loafers matched his pants. *This brotha is weird*, she thought. He was in deep thought, quiet - too quiet. Yasmina watched him rest his forehead lightly against his hand. She wondered how he came to be the person to help her. Or, was he with the people who threatened her using Serosa while she sat on death row?

The questions nagged Yasmina until she couldn't stand it any longer.

"Jesus!" she blurted out, causing the man's head to lift from its resting position.

The silence inside the car was too much as they'd been driving for twenty minutes without one word. Pivoting in her seat, Yasmina grabbed the man's sleeve, tugging at it so furiously he almost lost his balance. "Excuse me!" she spat, her tone full of sarcasm. "Hello, you could say something to me you know. At least tell me where the hell we're going." For a moment, the man stared at Yasmina. He didn't speak, only stared. Yasmina rolled her eyes and let out a deep sigh.

"Look here, damn it!" she cursed, fed up with the games. "I'm going to irritate the hell out of you until you talk to me, tell me something." She grabbed his arm again. "Don't just sit there and ignore me when I'm asking you questions." Her words were sharp and precise; in Yasmina's mind, she'd gotten her point across when the man turned to face her. He touched the tip of his glasses with his finger and sighed.

"Who I am is not important," he said with a heavy British accent. His demeanor was calm. He moved slowly like he owned time and leaning back against the seat, he continued. "All you need to know is ….," he paused then added, "…we're taking you somewhere safe, and once there, you are to await further instructions." Just like that the conversation was over. The brotha resumed his former stance, facing the window and resting against his hand. As Yasmina watched him act like nothing happened, she was beyond belief. *Uh-uh! No this fool didn't just dis me like I'm nobody,* Yasmina thought to herself. *You piece of shit. The first chance I get I'm bailing on you.*

The man made an abrupt move, one he would regret.

"What the bloody hell are you doing?!" The man regained his composure after finally being able to pry Yasmina's sharp nails from his skin. "I was only reaching for this." He held a cell phone in his hand. "It's a burner, a disposable cell phone."

After seeing the small phone, a sheepish expression crept over Yasmina's face. "Sorry," she whispered, a smirk creasing her lips. The coquettish apology didn't work. "You will be receiving a call in a few days or so. Don't call anyone from this phone," he snapped at Yasmina. Listening to this stranger bark orders, Yasmina could tell by his accent that he'd either studied English in school or picked up phrases from books or television. The way he pronounced certain words made her grimace, even though she found the accent attractive.

As they rode along in silence, she studied the phone. It was no bigger than the palm of her hand and as she recalled the phone she had ten years ago, she was surprised at how much technology had advanced while she was incarcerated. Yasmina turned in the brotha's direction. "You still haven't answered my questions. Where am I? Where are you taking me? Who are you?"

This caused him to laugh. He couldn't take it anymore. Yasmina frowned, sensing she was becoming the butt of a joke she knew nothing about.

"What's so funny?"

"Are all American women as feisty and as blunt as you are?"

This time it was Yasmina who couldn't hold back her laughter. As she eyed the man, they both chuckled knowingly, it was then that her earlier anxieties began to fade and she started to relax. The man also opened up. "Honestly, I shouldn't be divulging this information to you, but you're in Switzerland." Removing the glasses from his face he added, "I'm Giddeon, and where I'm taking you I won't share; it's better that you don't know - for your safety of course."

Yasmina opened her mouth to speak only to be interrupted.

"If it eases your mind any, I'm a friend of Damita's."

Hearing the name mentioned brought a smile to Yasmina's face. To know Damita had her hand in on this was comforting, and it showed that Damita was with her to the end. "What?" asked Giddeon of Yasmina's smile.

"Nothing," Yasmina replied adding, "Only something that's crossed my mind." She was too embarrassed to share the thought. Instead, she let her eyes roam across the beautiful landscape of the Swiss Alps.

Yasmina never knew how beautiful nature could be until now, but as quickly as the thought came, it went when the car came to a screeching halt in front of an empty building.

CHAPTER TWO

GENEVE, SWITZERLAND
7:37 A.M.

"What's this?" asked Yasmina as she frowned at the run down building. Giddeon refrained from speaking. He was busy glancing over his shoulders, taking in his surroundings.

"Come quickly," he said as he grabbed her wrist to leader her through traffic.

They were in the Red Light District, the center of Switzerland's sex pot, and a place where many came to enjoy rest, relaxation, and beautiful women from all over the country. Along the strip were brothels, legalized prostitution dwellings, and drug spots. Yasmina's journey to the district wasn't fun or for enjoyment. As she stood in a dark corner, she was repulsed watching the whores stop in alleyways or some shady spot beside a building to perform sexual acts. Yasmina suddenly felt nauseous; the sight brought on memories of being violated while in prison. She gagged, doubling over with sharp pains of anxiety piercing her insides.

Before ever coming to the place, Yasmina had heard so much about it. The way people spoke of its beauty, describing it as one of the most breath-taking countries in the world, she couldn't wait to visit. But now, as she eyed the remnants of what centuries of government misappropriation of funds and taxes left behind, she learned a lesson in history she never imagined.

This place isn't any different than Jamaica and other poverty-stricken countries.

The thought saddened Yasmina as she stood gripping the side of the door. It wasn't until Giddeon tugged at her sleeve when she realized she'd lost track of time staring at people.

They entered a hallway. It was so small, only one person could walk through at a time. Yasmina's mind started to wander as she followed Giddeon, wondering how long she would have to be in this place. They rounded a corner adjoining another hallway before Yasmina stopped dead in her tracks. Standing right before them was a small girl who looked to be no older than twelve. Something about the girl disturbed Yasmina, something she couldn't quite put a finger on. When Giddeon realized Yasmina was a further behind than she should have been, he turned on his heels.

"Come on," he grabbed her by the arm leading her past the girl. "The room is just up ahead."

Yasmina was restless; she couldn't get comfortable in a strange room. She paced back and forth. A few times she thought about sneaking out, but quickly dismissed the idea with Giddeon's warning in the back of her mind.

"Whatever you do," he had said, "do not step outside this door once I leave the room. If you need food, I'll bring it; the same goes for personal hygiene. These people here care only about one thing - money - and if they feel you can bring some in for them they'll drug you and put you on the streets with the rest of these whores."

In the beginning, when Yasmina first learned that she would be hidden away at a safe house, a smile came to her face. When she learned that the hideaway was in Switzerland, the place where she held her bank accounts netting in millions, she got even more excited. That excitement didn't last long.

For moments she stood in the middle of the room with nothing to do until her eyes landed on a piece of soiled fabric. The cloth now in her hand, she wiped in circles against the windowpane until the dust left a haze clear enough to see through. What Yasmina saw in front of her brought back painful memories: Rue de Berne.

The strip was long; it reminded Yasmina of Grand Concourse Avenue in the Bronx, or the strip of Collins Avenue in South Beach. People packed the street and businesses both legal and illegal were a fixture to this society. She watched the destruction of a society that somewhere along the line got lost in government corruption, pimps, dealers, addicts, and prostitutes. Yasmina realized that this place was like many she'd visited before. As if this revelation wasn't enough, Yasmina was caught off guard when she heard something just outside her door.

"Qi est le cest dub le, cal pute?"

("Where is the rest of the money, you little bitch?")

Yasmina tensed. Even though the man spoke broken French, she had a pretty good idea of what he said. Tip-toeing to the door, she pressed her eye to the peephole. In what appeared to be a more controlled tone, Yasmina watched as he scolded someone, not able to make out who was being cursed at. Once the man stepped aside, Yasmina realized it was the young girl she'd seen earlier.

"Frans, that is all of it." The girl started shaking as the man stood over her. Her English was broken, but Yasmina managed to figure out what she was saying. "The one gentleman, the fat, chubby, smelly guy, he refuses to pay saying I didn't succeed in pleasuring him. He said he speak with you about the money."

Yasmina's heart ached as she listened to the explanation. It pained her to know that a child so young was forced to live in such a way. It was unbearable to see the fear in the girl's eyes as she tried to shield herself from another blow from the man. There was nothing she could do; Yasmina was in no position to help anyone. She was a wanted fugitive hiding out in another country and if anyone was to learn of this, back to prison she went. Realizing the danger of her situation, Yasmina stepped away from the door, but something pulled her back. Quickly she looked back through the peephole and what she saw caused a sigh which she stifled by placing both hands over her mouth. Blood had begun to trickle from the corner of the girl's mouth and both of her eyes were swollen. To hear her plead with this man to give her until later that night to recover the lost funds tugged at Yasmina's motherly heartstrings. She could only lie on her bed and think of the hardship Serosa endured over the last ten years. This was something that disturbed her when first encountering the girl.

CHAPTER THREE

Bored out of her mind, Yasmina walked around the room. Three long days had come and gone and the only entertainment was an outdated floor-model television set with little-to- no clarity and a novel Giddeon left - *Wretched of the Earth*.

There were many times she thought about grabbing the cell phone and making a quick call, so the day the cell phone rang, it didn't take long for Yasmina to flip it open and answer.

"Hello?!" she shouted.

Seconds passed before the person finally answered. "Yes, is this you?"

The voice was familiar; it was like music to her ears. Yasmina thought her journey was finally coming to an end. As she pondered this and what her future would be, she began to smile. She glanced around the room as if it would be the last time she would ever see the place. Knowing her trusted friend had come through for her so many times, Yasmina fought to contain the excitement she felt.

"My God, I thought this day would never come! I mean, I can't begin to tell you how thankful I am for everything you've done for me. Taking my daughter in…"

Yasmina was so excited she didn't notice Damita trying to get a word in. It's wasn't until Damita shouted, "Please, Yas, just listen for a second!" that Yasmina finally shut up. "Damita, what is it?" asked Yasmina, sensing trouble.

"I have some bad news," Damita sniffled through tears streaming down her face. "I don't know if you can handle what I'm about to say."

After listening to the heart wrenching news, Yasmina got dizzy. She collapsed on the bed, her mind swirling, spinning out of control. She felt as if she was in the middle of the ocean, the undercurrent dragging her down.

"How could this be?" she cried questioning no one in particular. "Not my Serosa, Shotty Dread!" she cried. "I thought he was locked away in prison."

Yasmina was abruptly brought out of her grief when a bone-curdling laugh that she was all too familiar with sounded in her ear.

"Yasmina, we meet again," Shotty Dread chimed. "Sounds like me catch you by surprise," he said. His voice then took a serious tone.

"Dere's a lot we 'ave ta settle, and the sooner the betta."

The moment Yasmina heard the voice her heart sank. She knew making idle threats to a man like Shotty Dread was a waste of time, he killed merely for the enjoyment of watching people suffer. Instead of browbeating him with intimidation, she elected to agree with his demands. As thoughts came to mind of what Shotty Dread had done to her grandmother, Rosa, and best friend, Selena, Yasmina got sad. Again, the actions and lifestyle she'd lived a decade ago were about to unleash fury on innocent people. Once again, it would be people Yasmina loved who would die at the hands of Shotty Dread.

Yasmina had finally found her voice. She was about to speak up, when Shotty Dread cut her off, "It's in your best interest to leave dem bumble clot police outta dis!"

The dial tone buzzing in her ears was a reminder of what was to come in the next few days.

CHAPTER FOUR

Minutes passed as Yasmina lifted herself from the bed. Moving beside the window, she parted the ragged set of Venetian blinds. There was a crowd of people gathered on the Rue de Berne.

For as long as Yasmina could remember, in one aspect or another, her life had been controlled by someone, first it was Shotty Dread, who chased her and Scorcher from Jamaica to Florida. Then, she was confined to a prison cell for ten years of her life only to be told when to do certain things, and to be mistreated like she was an animal.

Now, as her eyes moved up and down the crowded block watching people move about, she made up her mind. *I'll be damned if I'm going to let Shotty Dread, or anyone for that matter, dictate my happiness.* As the thought went through her head, her eyes took in each person milling around. There was one in particular she hoped to find and after minutes of searching and coming up empty handed, Yasmina sighed. She'd just released the long string that hoisted the blinds when her eyes caught movement. The gesture was faint, almost unnoticeable. If it weren't for the small trinket, a red bracelet-like band wrapped around the girl's wrist, Yasmina would've missed her. Straining her eyes, she watched as the girl motioned to an older gentleman. Yasmina's mind immediately went into survival mode.

Three loud knocks at the window pane didn't get the girl's attention because she was engrossed in conversation. Loud noise from drivers and pedestrians didn't help the matter. Once again, Yasmina was back to where she began - nowhere.

She tried again to get the girl's attention. With her hand wrapped tightly around the base of the cord, Yasmina viciously jerked, nearly causing the blinds to topple to the floor. It worked. The girl's head abruptly turned in the direction of the movement. Squinting her eyes for seconds, she watched the window only to find what appeared to be the curtains shifting. The man she was with, a possible client, was clearly angered by her neglect. He sighed and stormed off in another direction. Things seemed to be looking brighter as Yasmina watched the girl slowly and nonchalantly move in her direction. Her happiness was almost uncontrollable as she shifted from one foot to the other. The girl had closed the distance, now only a few feet away, but, as quickly as the excitement grew, alarm followed.

"Noooo!" Yasmina screamed, seeing the girl's steps become more doubtful the closer she advanced. When it was apparent the girl had second thoughts, nearly turning away, Yasmina yelled, "Don't go, please!"

Though her voice echoed around the room, it didn't break through the glass pane. Yasmina cringed in defeat when the girl completely turned her back. She tried one last time to get the girl's attention. The hard thud almost shattered the glass. The blinds now lay in crumpled heap at Yasmina's feet, but she succeeded in what she set out to do. After regaining the girl's attention, Yasmina desperately waved both hands mouthing, "Come here!"

Again the girl squinted, this time putting her hand over her eyes like a visor. The outside of the window panes were filthy, just like the inside panes when Yasmina first moved into the room. It was disgusting, but the girl did see a hand vigorously waving from side to side. She smiled at the thought of a potential client. The girl's pace quickened. She now stood directly at the ledge of the window. When realizing it was a female beckoning her, the smile turned into a frown and she didn't hesitate to redirect her steps. Yasmina noticed the expression also. She also knew that once the girl moved on, her chances of ever gaining the upper hand would be lost. She did the inconceivable.

The fresh air was inviting. The second Yasmina stepped through the door a blast of fresh air met her. Her lungs expanded. Her nostrils flared welcoming in new life, something she hadn't felt in days. To see passing cars, horns honking, people chatting, engines roaring was overwhelming, but Yasmina wasn't there to enjoy freedom. She was outside braving danger for a more important agenda, Serosa's life.

Yasmina's eyes immediately went to the lamppost. It was the place she'd first spotted the girl, but it was empty. Yasmina panicked, her heart fluttered.

"Where did she go?" her question was lost in the loud honking of a driver speeding by.

For seconds she stood heartbroken, her eyes quickly flashing in each direction. She was in a world very far from the one she'd known, a wilderness that didn't offer any insight to her situation or any answers of how to turn it all around. There was only fresh air and the noise of people going about their day.

Yasmina was disappointed by the fact that she blew what little chances she'd had in finding a way to regain control of her situation. She was about to give up when something startled her.

"Stop! Lady, stop!" two men screamed at the top of their lungs.

The men were very anxious. One wore a white garb draped over his body and stood no taller than five feet. The other was tall and lanky, with a long beard.

Hearing people call out to her, Yasmina casually looked behind her but no one was there. She turned back to find the men now moving through traffic toward her. Yasmina knew this meeting wasn't coincidental. It was something Giddeon warned her about. Now, as she watched in horror as the men gained ground, she tried to figure out what to do. *Run!* her mind instinctively shouted.

In Yasmina's confused state, she watched as cars came to a screeching halt to avoid hitting the men. As adrenaline pumped through her body, she knew escaping shouldn't have been a problem, but her legs wouldn't move. Clumsily, Yasmina reached behind her, searching for anything to latch on to, something that would aid in freeing her from this invisible force. The men shouting sent chills through her body. She tried to take a few steps back when a strong hand clutched her shoulders. She froze.

A voice shouted, "Come this way. Inside!"

It didn't take long for Yasmina to gather herself. Besides, she was practically being dragged by the arm as the girl led her through the dark hallway. They safely made it to a strange building. Standing at the door, a bewildered expression came to Yasmina's face as something dawned on her.

"My key!" she yelled, frantically groping the pockets on her pants.

The girl watched in confusion. Yasmina desperately fumbled every placed on her body a small key could be placed, but it was nowhere to be found.

Both men had cleared traffic. They were held up on the sidewalk glancing left and right as their eyes searched up and down the crowded street. Fearing they'd lost a potential employee, the tall bearded man said, "Here, let's check the building."

Yasmina felt like her heart would beat through her chest. Her hands trembled. Her knees knocked. Her body shook uncontrollably. For seconds she stood with her back against the door, her breathing shallow, as she feared exhaling too loud would give away her position.

As she and her new accomplice remained silent, both eying each other, there was mutual understanding between them both. They made it, barely. Seconds passed before either Yasmina or the girl moved. Gazing through the peephole in the door, Yasmina released a huge sigh when finding no one outside the room door. The girl looked through the peephole and watched the men crossing back through traffic.

"Ils s'en vont." She pointed through the curtain.

Yasmina shrugged her shoulders, her face masked with confusion.

The girl smirked. "They…they are leaving," she stammered, "Crossing the street."
When making it over to the bed, she collapsed on her back. While thinking of the brush she'd just had, something registered in her mind causing her to jump.

"Where did you get that from?" Yasmina questioningly eyed the girl. The young girl saw the frown on Yasmina's face and shied away.

"Ici une seule cle ouvre toutes les portes des chambers." She gestured with both hands up at her sides, her shoulders hunched.

"Uh-uh!" Yasmina quipped moving closer to the girl. "A few seconds ago your ass was speaking perfectly broken English. Now all of a sudden you wanna speak French."

The young girl moved near Yasmina. Fishing back into her pocket, she withdrew the key, handing it over to Yasmina, a sheepish grin on her face.

"One key opens every room door in this place."

Even though Yasmina was grateful for the girl's honesty, the thought of what she'd just learned frightened her. She grabbed the young girl's hand, shaking it.

"Thanks anyway," Yasmina smiled. "If it weren't for you, I'd be up shit creek without a paddle, if you know what I mean."

The girl shook her head. She didn't understand.

"Never mind," said Yasmina. "You have a lot to learn about America."

CHAPTER FIVE

Yasmina couldn't restrain herself. She'd been doubled over with laughter for the last few hours. She was held up inside the room with young Liddy since the ordeal with the two men earlier that day. And the things she was learning about Liddy had her full of humor.

"...and this guy," Liddy said, gesturing with her hands, "a real fat swine of a pig, he says, come bebe, that's right, come bebe, it's getting there...uh-uh...I'm almost there....that's it...keep going."

Yasmina couldn't believe what was coming from the girl who was no older than twelve years of age. She continued listening as Liddy finished. "He couldn't keep an erection so he didn't pay me. He said it was my fault."

Immediately as the last words came, Yasmina remembered the incident outside her room door. Her expression turned serious.

"And Frans..." Yasmina questioned, "You say he's your uncle?"

Liddy's expression turned from excitement to sadness. The smile that once was etched across her face had disappeared.

"He's a piece of shit is what he is!" Liddy angrily spat.

After explaining about her mother being bedridden from an unexplained sickness, she said, "You see we cannot afford a doctor, and ma-ma has to remain in bed. Her legs swell the size of a futbol."

"What about your father, or brother? You have any other relatives?" asked Yasmina, whose heart ached with pain for Liddy. A gloomy expression covered Liddy's face. Noticing this, Yasmina also saw a hardness in the girl's face and began to wonder just how long had she been in this predicament. Her question was answered shortly afterward.

"My pa-pa died two years ago, a heart attack," Liddy said as she moved toward the window. Her gaze was far away. "My younger brother, Anselemn, he died a month after pa-pa, an illness doctors said they had no name for claimed him."

The words hit Yasmina hard. She watched as a tear slid from Liddy's eye, which she hid by quickly wiping it with her hand. She continued.

"So, you see, with my ma-ma being sick, I have to provide food to eat and money for medicine so that she can get well."

Yasmina couldn't hide the fact that her throat was on fire. She'd done everything - opened her mouth, swallowed, even cleared her throat, but the tears came. What she'd learned within the past few hours was heart wrenching. After dabbing a few tears from her face, Yasmina moved near Liddy. With her hand gently resting on her shoulder, Yasmina eyed the door.

"That man," she pointed down the hallway, "Your Uncle Frans," Liddy nodded her head anticipating more. "How much money does he give you?"

Liddy jerked away from Yasmina's grip.

"He takes care of my ma-ma."

Yasmina was furious. She couldn't believe the audacity of her uncle, even though she didn't know him. *How could he prostitute his own niece?*

On one hand, Yasmina wanted to embrace Liddy, to let her know that things would get better but the truth of the matter was Yasmina knew Liddy wasn't facing a situation that would improve overnight. What she was going through would take days, weeks, months, even years before things got any better. The reality was the situation could never change.

The room had a black cloud hanging over it. Yasmina came to the realization that if she was going to change her own situation, she had to redirect the discussion. Reaching inside a bag sitting beside the nightstand, Yasmina pulled out a wad of cash. Liddy's eyes got big. Yasmina peeled of a twenty dollar bill and held it out.

"Gun!" she blurted, the words rolling off her tongue slowly. Liddy was confused.

Seeing this, Yasmina yelled, "Gun. Pow!" She gestured with her fingers.

The once blank expression on Liddy's face turned into a smile. "Gun. Pow! Pow!" Yasmina teased. "Oh, you wan' a gun to kill somebody....maybe Uncle Frans?" Liddy smirked. Yasmina laughed and gave Liddy five extra twenties. "I'll have more for you when I get what I want."

CHAPTER SIX

At mid-morning and while sound asleep, Yasmina was awakened by an abrupt sound. Someone was knocking on the door. Stunned, she quickly glanced at her watch realizing it was nearing 6 a.m.

For the past few days, Giddeon had been bringing her the bare necessities to make it through the day, food and hygiene products. She sighed and dragged herself to the door.

The face Yasmina saw standing before her was a nightmare come true. She panicked and tried to slam the door, but the strange man was too strong. His face had three-day-old stubble. A black do-rag covered his head, the strings hanging on each side of his face. There were two gold caps covering his front teeth but what frightened Yasmina the most was his strength. He didn't seem to exert much energy as he leaned his shoulder into the door, wedging it open.

Yasmina quickly went into survival mode. She knew that she was much weaker than this man. She had to think fast if she was going to make it out alive.

The man let out a loud scream as Yasmina's teeth latched onto his fingers. Releasing his grip on the door, he tried to grab a bag hanging around his neck.

"You got the wrong room!" Yasmina grunted. She was still trying to push the door shut when she realized the man's shoe was wedged between it and the frame.

The man wouldn't let up as his eyes lingered on her cleavage. "No," he shook his head, "I don't have the wrong room."

After making the comment, his eyes again brushed over the robe dangling off of Yasmina's shoulders. For an instant, he got aroused. When he recognized fear in Yasmina's eyes for the second time, he threw up a hand.

"One minute." He fumbled through the bag around his neck. When he felt he had what he needed, he uttered,

"This is what you wan' for." He pulled out a small caliber gun.

Seeing the gun caused Yasmina's heart to pound. "Liddy, she tell me a lady in this room want a gun." When Yasmina heard this, she calmed down.

The stranger put the black duffle bag on the bed. "I'm Chabaaga." He extended a hand to Yasmina as she stared at him.

"If you were in America and pulled a stunt like the one you just did, you would've gotten your hand blown the fuck off."

"Excuse-moi?" Chabaaga questioned, not understanding what she meant.

Yasmina sucked her teeth. There was no point in trying to explain, she was sick and tired of this place. She was being hidden from everyone with no possible way of knowing the welfare of her daughter, except through the person who was holding her hostage. She'd been chased by strangers for no apparent reason and, she was forced to live in a shitty, abandoned hotel that reeked of stale and musty air in one of the roughest places in Switzerland. She only wanted to handle her business with Shotty Dread and get the hell out of there.

One by one Chabaaga pulled weapons out of the bag. He tried making small talk.

"You know, I tink Jay-Z and G-Unit are two of the best rappers in da game."

Yasmina laughed.

When she didn't respond to the comment, Chabaaga changed topics.

"Dis one here," he pointed to an all black weapon, "is a .380 Lorcin. It holds seven in da magazine and one in da chamber." His eyes fixed on Yasmina before moving on.

"Okay, dis one is something you can conceal and it will do damage. It's a .25 automatic."

Yasmina's silence was enough to convey her disapproval. She shook her head. "Look, if that's all you came with then you've wasted a trip. I'm looking for something that'll insight fear in a muthafucka just by seeing it. I ain't got time for some little…" Her mouth fell open when Chabaaga pulled the next weapon out of the bag.

"This is what I'm talkin' `bout!" Her fingers slid across the .40 Caliber Desert Eagle.

Staring at the gun, memories of Latoya, her ex-Platinum Chick member, flashed through her. Yasmina snapped back when Chabaaga grabbed the weapon. "No! No!" He gently placed the huge gun back inside the bag.

"What? Why can't I have it?" Yasmina asked. Her wrinkled brow told of her disappointment.

Fluffing the bags as if he'd placed a delicate, priceless artifact inside, Chabaaga said, "Dis weapon, someone else already placed an order."

"Forget that!" blurted Yasmina. "I'm willing to pay double what that other person is going to give you."

For seconds Chabaaga contemplated the offer. Reaching back inside the bag, he removed the same gun.

"It will cost you a great deal."

Without hesitating, Yasmina walked over to a bag sitting beside her bed.

"Here!" she tossed a neat stack of bills into his hand. "I know your people ain't paying more than five grand, but that's ten thousand dollars right there if you let me get those other two along with this one."

Chabaaga stared at the money like it was gold. "Is there anything else I can do for you, maybe some marijuana or coke?"

Yasmina chuckled and Chabaaga smiled.

"Yeah," she eyed him seriously. "There is one more thing you can do." After telling him to get her another burner, Yasmina was surprised when Chabaaga walked over to the television set in the middle of the room.

"You've read that book?" Yasmina asked as Chabaaga picked up the book.

"No, this is what Liddy told me to look for when I knocked on the door." Yasmina's facial expression told that she didn't understand until Chabaaga added, "She said if I didn't see da big red book on top of the t.v., I had the wrong room."

CHAPTER SEVEN

Time seemed to be the only good thing Yasmina had on her side. An entire day had passed since the ordeal with Chabaaga, and her patience was wearing thin.

It was after midnight when she finally decided to settle down. With the same red book *Wretched Of The Earth* clutched tightly in her hands, Yasmina had just positioned her head against the backboard of the bed, a soft pillow resting at the base of her neck, when the burner given to her by Giddeon, rang.

She jerked, her body abruptly springing forward.

Yasmina's eyes went to the table the phone was sitting on. She glanced at her watch. The phone was now on its second ring when a thought came to her.

This could be only one of three people, Damita, Shotty Dread or Giddeon.

Yasmina figured it was Giddeon as she pressed the send button.

"You sure know the right hour to check on a woman, Giddeon," she teased, a huge smirk on her face.

Yasmina couldn't help thinking of how professional Giddeon attempted to be during their first encounter. She found him hilarious. Since then, he'd subtly flirted with her in his own way, something that managed to bring a smile to her face.

After long moments of silence and no response, her smile disappeared.

"Hello?" she shouted again, anger registering in her tone. "Giddeon, stop playing."

She froze after an unfamiliar voice interrupted her.

"Call this number, 202-555-9634 at 3:00 P. M. today, not a second later."

The loud sound of the phone clicking and stinging of the dial tone buzzing in her ear sent a bone-curdling chill through Yasmina. She couldn't erase the icy tone. The man's voice was confident; he sounded like he was certain he could touch her anytime he felt the need. Yasmina jumped out of bed and grabbed the Desert Eagle she just bought. She racked the chamber and pressed her body against the wall. Yasmina edged closer to the window and separated the blinds with the long barrel of the gun to do a quick survey of the area.

Rue de Berne held nothing out of the ordinary. Yasmina was even stunned to find the place as busy in the wee hours of the morning as it was in broad daylight. A part of her expected to find some stranger standing right outside her window announcing he was guilty of making the call. There was one thing she was certain of: this anonymous caller's reason for trying to scare Yasmina would only be explained if she called him at 3:00 P. M.

CHAPTER EIGHT

No matter how hard Yasmina tried, she couldn't erase the voice from her head. It unnerved her to know someone, a total stranger, had gotten a number that only Damita, Giddeon and Shotty Dread knew. Yasmina felt as if she were a puppet dangling from a string in a show where criminals were the masters of ceremony. She walked back to the window and peeked through the blinds. She scanned the entire block, trying to pinpoint signs of the intruder. Though it was early morning and she'd had little sleep, she was determined to find the bastard who was trying to intimidate her. She watched for seconds as an older man inserted a small key into a lock and entered the building.

Her eyes then roamed to a short Jewish man who was busy setting up his news and magazine kiosk.

Just as Yasmina moved to return to her bed, she saw something in the corner of her eye. It was Liddy! She ushered a gentleman wearing a dark suit into the foyer of another abandoned hotel situated directly across the street. Seeing this young girl being forced into prostitution saddened Yasmina, but there were other things to worry about. Yasmina had to protect Serosa and herself.

The huge slab of wood creaked as Yasmina slowly twisted the door knob. T he sound reminded her of the home she lived in Kingston with her parents. Once the door was opened wide enough, she jutted her head out, her eyes curiously searching up and down the small, unlit hallway.

As Yasmina stood timidly outside the door, thoughts of what happened the day before with the two men crossed her mind. She fingered the huge Desert Eagle and clutched it tightly to her chest. After finding nothing suspicious enough to serve as a threat, she retreated back into the room. Stress combined with fear and sleep deprivation consumed her the second she sat on the bed. She fell asleep, the gun grasped tightly in her hand.

Giddeon arrived later in the day around 2:30 P.M. His arms were full of bags of food, personal hygiene items and two books. After unloading the bags, Giddeon turned toward Yasmina with a smile until his eyes settled on something.

"Nice gun!" The smile quickly turned serious. "You expecting trouble?"

The question caught Yasmina off guard causing her to thrust it under a pillow. For a moment she wondered if she should tell him about all the shit that happened - being chased by two men, and the phone call. Giddeon beat her to the punch.

"You can't deny there's something on your mind, wanna talk about it?"

Yasmina looked out of the window. "I received a call from some guy earlier."

"Okay," Giddeon smiled. "When do you expect to see your daughter?"

Watching Yasmina shake her head from side to side made Giddeon frown suspiciously.

"What are you not telling me, Yasmina?"

In one swift movement, he withdrew two guns from under his arm. His eyes closely following Yasmina, Giddeon slowly unlatched the flimsy chain lock on the door. After a quick glance outside, he re-entered the room. After fastening the lock back, he stopped beside the window and peered through the blinds. Giddeon was uneasy; something wasn't right. In their present situation, there were two things Giddeon knew to be certain: some stranger had called the burner, and he couldn't have covered his tracks as well as he thought after picking Yasmina up from the airport. After realizing that there was no immediate danger, he sat beside Yasmina.

"What did the man sound like? Did he have an accent? What did he say?"

The rapid fire questioning started to irritate Yasmina. She too wondered how the stranger got the number.

"He didn't leave a name, never mentioned why he was calling – nothing." her frustration was apparent. "The only thing he said was it would be in my best interest to call this number," she held a piece of paper up, "by 3:00 P.M. today."

Giddeon looked at his watch, he realized they had less than half an hour to make the call and a thought came to mind.

"Did you make any calls from this phone?"

Yasmina's head jerked upward. Her eyes lit.

"No!"

Giddeon wasn't convinced, he kept asking questions. "Have you called anyone at all since you've been in this room?"

Yasmina raised herself from the bed. "I told you I didn't call--"

Immediately Giddeon saw Yasmina's face fall; he already knew the answer.

"Damnit!" he cursed. The abruptness caused Yasmina to cringe, her eyes widening in alarm.

As best she could, she tried shrinking into the covers. She wanted to hide how ridiculous she felt for letting him down.

"I only wanted to hear her voice," she cried, tears dripping from her eyes. "My baby, Serosa, I only wanted to tell her I love her." Yasmina's words trailed off as she buried her face into the pillow.

"Look," Giddeon knelt beside her, his voice soft and apologetic. "I didn't mean anything by cursing at you." Cupping her chin, his eyes met hers. "You have to understand something. In order for me to protect you and keep you safe, I have to know everything, and there are rules you have to follow if I'm going to achieve this. You must realize how important it is for you to remain hidden, that means no venturing outside that room and no outgoing calls."

As Yasmina listened, she began to feel better, but she really hadn't been completely honest. There was still the matter of the two men.

"Again," Giddeon replied, seeing that he managed to regain Yasmina's attention. "Did the man sound American or did he have an accent like mine?" After learning this much, he replied, "Good. Your daughter, Serosa, does she live at this number?"

Yasmina shook her head, "No."

Giddeon was deep in thought. Shaking his head, he replied, "That's not good."

They were seated side by side, neither aware of how long Giddeon's hand lingered on Yasmina's leg until she blurted out, "Area code, 202, if I'm correct, that's the area code for Washington, D.C."

Snatching his hands away Giddeon blurted, "You mean the place where the President of the United States lives? *That* Washington, D.C.?!"

Just as Yasmina opened her mouth to speak, a sound startled them. Someone was knocking at the door.

CHAPTER NINE

The knocks were earsplitting. They continued to come in succession, three raps at a time. Both Giddeon and Yasmina, with their weapons close to their bodies, eyed each other.

"Get on your knees," Giddeon whispered through clenched teeth. He was snaking his way along the wall as he inched nearer to the door. "And crawl inside the bathroom."

As Yasmina did this, the loud thuds sounded again, stopping her dead in her tracks. She turned her body, her worried eyes glancing at Giddeon. For moments an uncomfortable silence hovered in the room. As Giddeon racked his brain thinking of a means of escape, their chances seemed slim.

There was only one way out of the room - through the door. There wasn't an adjoining room in the old hotel and there were no bathroom windows. It was just a place for prostitutes to get a quickie with clients, or a refuge for people like Yasmina who needed to blend in with the crowd.

After a quick glance at his watch, Giddeon sighed. He realized time was running out to place the call. With his eyes locked onto Yasmina's and the slight gesture of the hand, he signaled, "five minutes," though his words never left his mouth. Both of them knew that their worst nightmare was about to come true.

Filling his lungs with air, Giddeon tightly gripped both weapons to his chest. His back plastered to the wall, adrenaline pumping viciously through his body, he braced himself and half-mumbled, "Here goes nothing." He pushed the doors open.

Yasmina was relieved to see Chabaaga standing at the door. After she explained to Giddeon how they met, everyone breathed a little easier.

"Okay," Giddeon grumbled. They weren't yet out of danger. "This is what I need you to do."

As Giddeon gave orders to both Yasmina and the man standing in front of him, he still couldn't believe this was happening. With all his might, he fought to suppress the anger that was building. Instead, he focused on the more important matter at hand - Yasmina's safety.

When Chabaaga received the instructions, he feverishly placed a call on his cell phone. He too had to stifle the anger he felt; once they'd squared things away with Yasmina, he and Giddeon would settle their score.

Moving next to Yasmina, Giddeon asked, "You know how to use that thing?

Without responding, Yasmina held the large weapon to the side, racking the chamber back. Once it slid forward locking the bullet in place, she smugly eyed Giddeon.

"I wouldn't have it if I didn't know how to use it."

"Well, just don't hesitate to pull the trigger if the need arises, and make sure you're pointing at the right target."

Yasmina could still detect indignation in Giddeon's voice. She wondered where it came from. Minutes earlier, when making the decision to confront whoever it was knocking on the door, Giddeon never thought it would be his nemesis, Chabaaga.

"What're you doing here?" Giddeon growled. He aimed both guns at the center of Chabaaga's chest.

Now that the two had unexpectedly come face to face again, the probability of someone dying was very high.

Speaking up for the first time, though he was staring down the barrels of two guns, Chabaaga spat, "I'm here on business. What's it to you, mate?"

Chabaaga's sarcastic tone didn't help the situation as Giddeon edged closer.

"Yeah," he chided, both guns resting underneath Chabaaga's chin. "And what business is that, mate?"

The hatred both men felt for each other was apparent. Yasmina didn't know either of them before coming to Europe, but she could tell there was deep-seated resentment between them. "You two know each other or something?" she asked. The answer she got was shocking.

"You see," Giddeon slowly moved back never taking his eyes off Chabaaga. "Last year I was told to contact this. . . Chabaaga. He's widely known through these parts of France as the go-to-guy when it comes to getting guns and drugs." "Well," he continued, "I needed him to broker a deal with a client from Saint-Denis, a ghetto located in Northeast Paris. I was willing to pay him a handsome amount of cash for his part but it just so happened that I got ripped off by a stick-up team of his." There was coldness in his eyes.

"Hold just a second, partna!" Chabaaga yelled inching closer to Giddeon. "You're busy blaming me for your bloody misfortune, who's to say you weren't the one who planned the entire thing? I mean, I lost out, too. I didn't get paid by you or your client, Orlandis. Second, my jewelry was taken, which I might add, cost me a fortune. If there's anybody to blame, it's you."

The argument had moved near the window. Yasmina, smaller than both men by at least four inches, moved in between them.

"Look guys, I'm not going to say who's right or wrong in what happened between the two of you but we all know that in this game, especially when dealing with money, no one's safe, and everyone's a target, sooner or later. The only thing you can do is count your losses and move on."

Yasmina's mind abruptly went back to when Latoya turned on her forcing her into a closet and robbed her. She was shaken from that memory when she heard glass break.

"What was that?" her eyes immediately landed on the shattered glass.

There was a lot of blood. The wound in Chabaaga's chest looked bad. His breathing was labored and his eyes rolled back in his head. Giddeon kneeled over the man he hated to watch him die. As Chabaaga lay drowning in his own blood, his mouth moved. His eyes fixed in a death gaze, he struggled to speak as blood poured out of his mouth. He died, his eyes wide open, the words that leaked from his mouth incomprehensible.

Giddeon eyed Yasmina.

"You have less than a minute to place the call."

CHAPTER TEN

The room was tight, the air was thick. Things were happening too fast. As Yasmina knelt behind the dresser in fear, she pressed the phone to her ear.

"Come on, damnit! Pick up, answer."

The desperation in her voice was apparent as she breathed into the receiver. She was almost a minute past her deadline when a voice uttered, "I thought you may have decided not to call, Yasmina."

Yasmina had no idea who the caller was or where he was calling from; it could have been just outside the building, or thousands of miles away in Washington D.C. The voice was slow, methodical and cold. She was in deep thought trying to figure out how the caller could've received information about her when the voice added, "I know a lot about you, Yasmina." She froze. He continued, "You were born in Kingston, Jamaica. You moved to Miami after the death of your parents. Your grandmother, Rosa, has been dead for the last ten years and you were shocked when you found out that it was the man you fell madly in love with who murdered your parents."

Yasmina got dizzy. Her head throbbed, spinning in a rapid motion. She wondered how this stranger could read off in chronological order events of her life that no one else had knowledge of.

"I know you're wondering who I am, right? How do I know things so personal? And," he paused, letting the words sink in. "You want to know what it is I want from you, right?"

"Yes," was all Yasmina could say.

"Good!" the stranger replied.

He had a way with words. He was very descriptive when he spoke, pronouncing words slowly. His tone carried a sense of self-assuredness and power, something that intimidated Yasmina.

"If the rest of this conversation is amiable, I can honestly say that we've made progress today, Yasmina."

Hearing this made Yasmina wonder, *What does this man think I can offer him?*

Her thoughts were answered when he said, "Just for starters, how I found you isn't what's important. Still, you need to know how serious this situation really is. I'm a professional and the people who work for me are professionals. They will go to great lengths to get what I want." After hesitating he added, "Your friend, the one who's probably dead from the chest wound, you see how easily it could've been you if I wanted you dead?"

The comment managed to hit a nerve in Yasmina. She glanced at Chabaaga's corpse.

"But, Yasmina," the caller continued, "I don't want to see you dead - at least not yet. To put it plainly, I'm giving you a chance to help yourself out of this situation."

Yasmina held a far-away look as she eyed Giddeon.

"What?" he mouthed, his words sounding foreign in her present state of mind.

Her nerves had been on edge ever since arriving at the strange place. She hadn't had a good night's rest, and the pressure of not being able to talk to Serosa was taking its toll.

"You're probably wondering why I'm not calling the authorities knowing your present status, right? Honestly,

Yasmina, you're more helpful to me out of prison than you are locked up." Yasmina breathed heavily into the phone as the caller continued to intimidate her.

"All it takes is one simple phone call and you will be waiting to have your death sentence carried out, but I don't think all that's necessary. Besides, if you ask me, ten years of hard time was more than enough punishment. Don't you agree?"

Yasmina remained silent. She hadn't even heard Giddeon calling out to her. She was in a time warp where everything stood still. There was no sense of direction, no reality, no way out of the horrifying dream she was living. The only thing real was the caller, and his next words.

"In exchange for your life, I want you to deliver something for me."

Yasmina wrinkled her face. What could possibly be so important that this stranger would resort to killing someone he didn't even know? When she learned what in fact he wanted delivered, her throat got dry. It was hard to breathe.

"I'll be calling you in exactly five days with a place to meet. We'll do the exchange there." The man paused again. "Yasmina, if you bring the authorities into this, you will die, I guarantee it."

When Giddeon saw distress on Yasmina's face, he embraced. For seconds tears were all she could manage. Cupping her chin in his hand, Giddeon lifted Yasmina's face to his.

"What did he want?" Yasmina fought back tears, "Serosa; he wants my baby." She crumpled into his arms, the emptiness in her words relaying how bad her heart ached.

CHAPTER ELEVEN

WASHINGTON, D.C.
Headquarters

The White House seemed busier today than most days. People shuffled from one end of the corridor to the other as meetings between joint chiefs-of-staff and other various government factions were held.

President L'Enfants was seated in the Oval Office, a place he was fast getting used to. It reminded him of a study, only this one was much nicer; there were marble floors shining with a bright gloss coat, antique furniture dating back centuries to when his forefathers ruled. He was in deep thought, his hands formed the shape of a triangle, his back resting against a plush leather swivel chair, his legs crossed at the ankles. It had been less than a month since he was elected commander- in- chief and the feeling left him overwhelmed. Things were falling into place. Soon he would be able to implement the plan he'd been working on nearly all his life.

Moments earlier, President L'Enfants had been visited by three of his top cabinet members to discuss a matter of foreign affairs. He couldn't have been e happier to see them leave. After releasing a huge sigh of relief, the President focused on the two remaining people who also desired his attention. They were seated across from him.

"I thought they handled this issue on the last President's watch?" he asked one of the individuals. After getting no answer, he asked, "Well, Leslie, what's so important about this situation that it couldn't wait until later this evening?"

Leslie Chudzinski was head of the CIA. She arrived minutes before the three cabinet members but was told to hold whatever information she had until the President finished his meeting.

One by one she removed what appeared to be photos from inside a black briefcase. Placing the pictures on the President's mahogany desk, she eyed him.

"These were received this morning." She shoved the 11x18 stills close to the President. "Interpol contacted my office after they were alerted by an air tow in France." President L'Enfants was silent, she continued. "An unregistered private jet was spotted landing at one of their private airfields yesterday and it was brought to our attention that this plane, a Lear jet of some sort, came from the United States."

The President was speechless. He fumbled through the contents, his face lacking expression.

"Leslie, I, I don't understand. What is it you're getting at?"

"Well, sir," she began. "This plane in question touched down at Le Bourget just outside of Paris. And it is believed, by facial recognition machines at Interpol, at least one or maybe some of the same people who'd escaped from the custody of federal agents were on that plane."

The allegations were serious. President L'Enfants moved away from the table. Adjusting his tie, he looked at the CIA director but didn't say a word. Though he realized that the fugitive was deemed armed and dangerous, he also knew that a country like France had more than enough resources and man power to apprehend this convict without the help of the United States.

For the first few days of President L'Enfants's term, after the story aired of Osei Love, an escaped convict, the president wanted to be known as a no-nonsense, aggressive and hard-nosed leader. When the opportunity arrived, he promised the public that he would chase this man down until they found him. He had suddenly forgotten that promise now that his position was secure. Sliding the photos away, the President said, "Leslie, I appreciate the update, and I'm confident that you will handle this matter. I have more important matters to deal with."

The President's attempt didn't bode well as she replied, "Sir, I don't think you understand." She slid the photos back before President L'Enfants. "Take a good look."

"Holy Christ!" President L'Enfants blurted out.

"What is it, sir?" asked Vice President Tinkerton, moving to his feet. It was the first time he'd spoken since entering the room.

President L'Enfants wasn't sure if he was more disturbed form the shock of what he'd just seen or the implication the CIA director made. *What did she mean by questioning how closely I looked at the photograph? Does she know something more than she's letting on or is she fishing?* he asked himself.

It wasn't until Tinkerton tugged at the President's sleeve mouthing, "Mr. President, are you alright?" that the President snapped out of his brief stupor.

"Nothing, uh, it's nothing," he said, not even bothering to glance in Tinkerton's direction.

Truth of the matter was that he was shocked to find Serosa in the picture. He knew that offering a convict, Sherry, the deal of a lifetime was a gamble. She promised that Serosa would die in prison. Now everything was jeopardized by the new information that Serosa was still alive.

"Mr. President, are you sure?" Leslie asked. "You do look a little flustered."

"You think maybe the escaped convict kidnapped this girl?"

The moment the words left his tongue, old memories came back to haunt him. President L'Enfants remembered it like it was yesterday. He, Dr. Carmichael, and a host of other physicians were gathered inside the room. With his arms folded across his chest, he watched as the doctor coaxed the frightened child onto the gurney.

Serosa was scared. She squirmed, flailing her tiny arms as she tried freeing herself from the leather restraints, her mind racing with memories of the first ordeal she'd undergone at the hands of the same people who stood before her. Her fighting was in vain; the straps were fastened tight. Again, she was the guinea pig for the Senator, now President of the United States, and his latest experimental drug - Cephazyrin 07N.

President L'Enfants's thoughts were broken when Leslie stormed form the office, the door slamming behind her.

"What's the latest on your project?" he asked Tinkerton, not bothering to glance in his direction. His eyes roamed the lush green grass across the White House lawn.

Tinkerton stood tall and strong, his shoulders were erect like a serviceman preparing for a ceremony. He was dressed in a new navy-blue suit, Armani, since his pay grade increased tremendously. He shot the President a glare.

Ever since Tinkerton became Vice President, things had been strained. On one hand he'd risen to a position no one expected him to be in, but now that he was there he had the idea that the President was trying to exploit him in a situation that could cost him his career, or worse, his life.

"Well, sir, the project you're inquiring about, the one you've had me working on the past few weeks, is still in the beginning stages."

President L'Enfants stared at Tinkerton as he continued to talk.

"I have a few men in Portland monitoring the house and as for the escaped convict, I'll immediately put more men on him with your permission, sir."

Again, President L'Enfants stared at Tinkerton.

"Adam, why do you keep insisting that I have knowledge of what you choose to do on your own time?"

When Tinkerton failed to reply the President added, "Never mind that; there is something I would like to know."

The question the President asked caught Tinkerton off guard. Moving across the room, he stalled for time as he tried to figure out the right answer to give L'Enfants.

Stopping just short of an antique chair sitting in the middle of the floor, he swallowed hard. Divulging every piece of information was a no-no. Dealing with someone as conniving as President L'Enfants, Tinkerton knew he had to be careful. As long as he kept the President on a need- to-know- basis, he'd have the upper hand if and when the need came, least he thought. The two eyeballed each other, each one trying to get the other to react. Neither spoke, they just stared. Then Tinkerton suddenly thought of something. It was the memory of a meeting he had had with the media. The engagement was unscheduled. President

L'Enfants was returning from a summit in Orlando and no one knew the exact time of his arrival. The place was filled with journalists and reporters who all wanted to get the President's reaction to the mortgage crisis and how it was going to be handled.

As things got more chaotic Tinkerton decided to use his position as Vice President to step in and calm everyone down, but that proved not to be his biggest obstacle.

President L'Enfants wasn't off the plane good when he stormed into Tinkerton's suite. "What gives you the right to make a speech on my behalf without conferring with me first?" The President was pissed; he couldn't even unbutton his coat because his hands were trembling so badly. Tinkerton had just put the phone on his desk and was about to settle into a book when the President barged in and started yelling.

"First of all, don't come in here without knocking, questioning me about the rights I have." The President was shocked by Tinkerton's tone.

"Secondly, those people were very adamant about what they wanted and you weren't here to tell them what they were asking to hear. No one could predict a time you were arriving and for what it's worth, I did manage to avoid a situation that could have otherwise turned ugly once the media placed their spin on it."

For seconds the President just stood in the middle of the floor. He felt so stupid for letting Tinkerton blackmail him into making him Vice President but as mad as he was at that very moment, he became resolved in the outcome. The situation could've been disastrous. He just couldn't let Tinkerton know how grateful he really was.

"You really need to realize something quick and fast." President L'Enfants grabbed the door knob and looked over his shoulder. "I'm the one who does all the talking in this house. You need to play by my rules. You got this position because of me and it can be taken just like that," he said as he snapped his fingers.

As Tinkerton looked beyond the beams of light shining through the opened door, he couldn't believe the audacity of the man in front of him.

"With all due respect, if you would just let me handle things the way I see fit, we'll have the results in no time. And if I'm correct, it was you who got yourself into this mess in the first place."

The President started to get out of his seat when Tinkerton added, "Before you go getting your pants all twisted up your ass, let me finish."

President L'Enfants belted out a hearty laugh. Though the chuckle was one filled with sarcasm, he knew having a cooler head would prevail when it came time to finish carrying out his plans.

Rising from his seat, President L'Enfants move around the desk. Placing a hand on Tinkerton's shoulder he said, "Son, if I'd known you had that much scrap in you when I first hired you, hell, I would've given you a different position a long time ago."

Tinkerton had just closed the door on his way out of the office when President L'Enfants muttered, "Everything happens in time, my boy, and your day will come soon." The door clicked shut.

CHAPTER TWELVE

PARIS, FRANCE
7:45 P.M.

Serosa stood on the balcony outside her hotel room. She gazed out at the landscape that stretched for miles- buildings, landmarks, statues, and monuments - all in a beautiful pattern that brought about the brilliance of the city. There was still sadness consuming her.

"Why does my life have to be so complicated?" she questioned aloud, though no one was there to answer.

Three days had passed. She and Brandon had been having problems. Even though the countryside offered peace and serenity, Serosa had a bad feeling that wouldn't go away. Something was about to happen.

"Baby, talk to me, "Brandon pleaded. "What's wrong?" Sucking her teeth, Serosa started to turn away when Brandon placed a hand on her arm.

"You would think that being in such a beautiful place would bring happiness but I can see that isn't the case."

For moments Serosa looked into Brandon's eyes, desperately wanting to respond. When she abruptly whirled out of his embrace to head back through the foyer leading into their spacious suite, he stood with his mouth open, shocked.

"I'm sorry, Brandon," Serosa whispered when Brandon kneeled beside her at the bed. "It's not you and I'm sorry if I'm being distant but we've been cooped up in this room for days. How much longer am I going to have to wait?"

Tears filled Serosa's eyes. Grabbing both of her hands, Brandon said, "Look, I can't sit here and pretend to know what you're feeling. All I know is I'm here with you no matter what happens. Besides, there's a lot at stake for all of us. You, me, Ms. Damita, your mom, but I can assure you of one thing: we're in this together."

As the words left Brandon's mouth, thoughts of what happened back in Portland flashed through Serosa's mind. The sound of a siren wailing in the distance drowned out any thoughts she had.

Serosa and Brandon were seven stories high. The continuous noise of more sirens blaring, this time sounding closer and closer, made them both go out on the balcony to see what was going on. Some police officers were forming barricades while bystanders gathered and other officers took up positions behind cars and at the corners of buildings. Brandon soon realized their troubles in Portland managed to find them thousands of miles away in Paris.

"Brandon!" Serosa shouted realizing whatever was happening really scared him. It wasn't until she yanked on his shirt when he said, "Uh, what? Did you say something?"

The confusion on his face caused her to take a second look.

"Damn!" she cursed after seeing the commotion below. "What's going on down there? There are a lot of police."

"You think. . .?" Serosa said when Brandon suddenly bolted for the room.

Naturally, Brandon's instincts kicked in. He was beside the bed now, cell phone in hand. Serosa, still trying to wrap her mind around what he was doing, watched as Brandon dialed a number.

"Who are you calling?"

Brandon didn't respond. He shifted back and forth on his feet.

Serosa's nerves began to tingle. Wringing her hands, she glanced below once more. This time when her eyes landed on the black sedan whose occupants were two gentlemen, her throat got dry.

"What is it, baby?" Brandon asked.

When Serosa didn't answer, not even turning to face him, he just continued to look over the balcony.

Brandon thought he saw a ghost; the white agent, Chief Sculea, whom he thought died from a gunshot wound to the chest, was standing below. Brandon almost dropped the phone.

"I thought he was dead," Serosa cried, her eyes searching Brandon's.

Without hesitating, Brandon pressed the send button to place the call again. He eyed Serosa.

"Go inside and pack. Now!"

For moments Brandon watched as the two men, followed by a small entourage of policemen, made their way toward the entrance of the hotel. Backing into the room, he waited as the phone rang. No answer.

"Damn it! Why isn't this muthafucka answerin' his phone?" Brandon paced back and forth.

Serosa, nervous, hastily stuffed articles of clothing into two bags.

"You think they're after us for what happened at Damita's?"

Brandon cut his eyes sharply at her. "What the fuck are you doing?" he cursed, not bothering to answer the question. "I told you one bag, not three." His nerves were shot, and his anger caused him to stomp toward Serosa. He jerked the bag from her hand dumping the contents on the bed. "We ain't got time for you to be packing an entire wardrobe. All that shit is gon' slow us down."

When realizing that the authorities were nearing their room, thoughts of what happened back in Portland swirled in his mind. His nerves had caused him to lash out at Serosa.

And now, as she shot a venomous stare at him, he realized his mistake.

"Listen, baby," he walked over extending his hand.

"Get the fuck away from me, Brandon." Serosa was pissed. He'd never yelled at her.

Slowly, and in silence, she began removing articles of clothing, flinging them each and every way. Then she stopped suddenly.

"Baby, what's wrong?" Brandon asked rushing over to her side.

Serosa was bent over in pain. The grimace on her face told of how excruciating it was.

She shook her head, jerking away from his grasp. "It's nothing. Let me finish what I was doing so I won't slow you down," she belted sarcastically. He'd just placed a hand on her wrist and was about to speak when something else caught his attention.

CHAPTER THIRTEEN

"Damn it, man!" Brandon cursed. He'd watched guest after guest make a hasty exit from their rooms. His face plastered to the peephole he said, "Them muthafuckas is moving e'ry body out 'cept us."

"What?" asked Serosa, only hearing part of the comment.

"Shhh!" Brandon gestured with a finger to his lips.

He was busy watching more and more people exit going down the hallway. He counted at least thirteen. Brandon's heart was pounding in his chest. He started to move when something in his periphery caused him to freeze. "I can see those two men, at least their backs." He whispered to Serosa, "It's them, baby, I'm certain of it."

Here was another situation Serosa wished they could've avoided. And now that was staring them in the face, it only added to the premonition she had earlier. Then, out of nowhere, the pain she'd felt moments ago was back.

"What is it, Serosa?" Brandon asked when noticing the jerking motions Serosa's body was making. She dry-heaved. "You're starting to scare me," he said with a concerned look on his face. Though Brandon's focus was on what was going on outside the room door, he was also concerned about what was happening inside the room. The unexplained bouts of pain, spasms, and dry-heaves worried him. After Serosa stood up, she placed her hand to her mouth, making a beeline for the balcony. She made it in time enough to vomit seven floors below.

The loud ring tone of Brandon's cell phone startled him. He completely forgot about what has happening outside of the room when Serosa ran for the balcony. It was on its second ring when he answered.

"Hello!" he snapped.

Before getting an answer the hotel phone rang, the red light flashing repeatedly. With the receiver of his cell phone still to his ear, Brandon shifted nervously. He knew the caller was more than likely Shotty Dread. The front desk was calling to verify that someone indeed occupied the room. As if this wasn't enough, Brandon was faced with another situation.

"We know you're in there," said a gruff voice as someone pounded on the door. "Come out! This is the police."

The demand was stern. If it wasn't so close and clear the threat wouldn't have meant as much as to Brandon but he knew this was serious.

"What we gon' do?" she asked Brandon. The pain she previously felt subsided as the threat grew closer. "We don't have any guns and, shit, if we did we could at least shoot our way out of this." Her expression was serious.

When the words left Serosa's mouth, Brandon couldn't help thinking how lucky he was to have her in his life. And though he wanted nothing else to do with the gangster lifestyle, his memory wouldn't let him forget the day Serosa saved his life in the face of danger as J.T. placed the gun beneath his chin. The reverie was short-lived as loud percussive noises emitted just outside the room. Someone was banging hard against a door.

"Sounds like you 'ave a lot goin' on 'round here." Shotty Dread's words were like heaven in Brandon's ears.

"Man, where the fuck you at?" cursed Brandon. He was pissed.

"You and your men did your dirt and left us hanging out to dry, huh?" Brandon exclaimed, feeling he would make known his frustrations. "You shoot two federal agents and then force us to another country while you claim to tie up a few loose ends. I guess we're the loose ends you meant."

Shotty Dread resented the comment and his tone reflected it when he said, "Rude boy, you know wha' you need, you need ta calm yer ass and slow ya roll."

After sensing he'd regained control of the conversation, Shotty Dread asked, "Now, what's the problem?"

Brandon explained everything. He talked about the police assembling barricades around the building, escorting pedestrians away and the snipers he watched take up positions in certain establishments across from the hotel. When Brandon couldn't come to a conclusion other than the fact that the police were coming for both he and Serosa, he sighed.

"Look, Mr. Shotty Dread, I don't know or understand the circumstances that happened between you and Serosa's mom, Yasmina, but I love her and she has nothing to do with the mess you have with her mother. Serosa has spent the last ten years of her life in the prison system and the only thing she wants is her mother." Brandon paused slightly catching his breath. He hadn't intended on holding such a deep conversation but seeing the state Serosa was now in, he felt compelled to speak from the heart.

"Are you gon' come and get us out of this jam?"

There was nothing but silence. Brandon thought somewhere along the line Shotty Dread had disconnected the call but when he heard what sounded like someone clearing his throat, he exhaled a sigh of relief.

"Man, look here," Shotty Dread finally said. "I don't 'ave time to talk about the history between myself and Yasmina, but, my intentions isn't what you tink."

"Are you gon' help us or not?"

After listening to Shotty Dread promised to help them, Brandon gathered their belongings. He then hurried over to Serosa who was doubled over in pain.

"Dang!" Brandon exclaimed, scared to death by what was happening with Serosa. He brushed back the hair that'd fallen over her clammy face. "Just try and hold on a few more minutes, ma. I'll have you out of here soon."

Outside the room the pounding was getting louder. Brandon could hear ordered being directed and every now and again stealing a glance through the peephole, he would see the silhouettes of the two men. He glanced at his watch.

"Come on, Shotty Dread!" he mumbled to himself, the pitiful cries of Serosa sounding in his ears. "Don't leave me hangin', man."

Although Brandon's main concern was getting Serosa out safely and to a doctor, the drama happening just outside the room door was just as important. Again, he glanced at his watch, his eyes going to his cell phone - nothing.

As his thoughts raced on what would happen once the police ran out of patience, the phone rang. Brandon grabbed it.

"A blue car is out-back waiting for you." It was Shotty Dread.

Brandon's heart rate slowed. He was thankful Shotty Dread had kept his word, but it didn't help the dilemma they still faced. He had to think fast.

"We can't exit through the front door, too many cops." Brandon's eyes locked on a window. It was located on the far side of the room, adjoining the kitchenette.

"This will have to do," Brandon mouthed to himself. He could see the car waiting below. "Now," he mouthed in an audible whisper, his eyes panning on Serosa, "I just gotta get Serosa to trust me."

As gently as he could, Brandon escorted Serosa over to the window.

"Baby," she said, her voice weak and pained, "Where we going?"

"Don't worry, baby," Brandon replied, though he too was worried. He'd taken his time to place Serosa against the wall while he fumbled with the window latch. He'd noticed the talking in the hallway had all but ceased.

"Serosa, we gon' have to be careful. I'm not sure how secure this fire escape is."

"Fire escape!" Serosa bolted upright, the pain that once had her bent over, had disappeared in her disbelief. Eying Brandon like he was a stranger, she said, "I'm not going out on no damn fire escape. Have you lost your mind? I'm dizzy enough as it is."

Brandon tried his best to fight the anger that was building. He knew their only chances of escaping were to use this route. He knew Serosa was sick but their freedom lay seven stories below and if it took descending an old and rusty ladder to ensure they escaped, that's what he planned to do.

Cupping Serosa's chin he said, "I know you're scared, but baby, it's our only way out. Shotty Dread has a car waiting below for us and if we're going to do it, we have to go now."

Serosa released a long sigh. She tried building her nerves. She'd just latched her foot over the window sill when both she and Brandon heard the room door crash in.

CHAPTER FOURTEEN

PARIS, FRANCE
6 hours later

The journey from Geneva to Paris had taken six hours. For Yasmina, it offered her time she needed to think about things. For the entire trip, her mind replayed over and over the words said by the anonymous caller.

"It's simple: a life for a life or both of you can die."

Just the mere thought of how desperate these people she was dealing with were at getting their hands on Serosa frightened Yasmina. *There's something more to all of this* ,she thought, though not realizing she'd really said the words. It wasn't until Giddeon asked, "What was that?" when Yasmina realized she had spoken aloud.

Yasmina shook her head. "It's nothing I was just thinking out loud."

Minutes later the car pulled off onto a nearby exit, coming to a stop in front of a building with drab signs and neon lights.

"Hotel I-bis," Yasmina struggled to pronounce.

Giddeon smirked.

"Ebis," he corrected, pronouncing the "I" as an "E." "It's called the Ibis Hotel." Pausing he added, "It's where you will be staying. The town is called Clinchy and we're on the North East side of Paris."

"Looks more like the ghetto to me," Yasmina snapped. Even though it was in the wee hours of the morning, she could clearly see the effects of what years of decay and lack of funding had done to the community. "I guess this is the part of Paris they don't tell you about in the news or the travel brochures, huh?"

Even though Giddeon was offended by the comment, he laughed.

"Sorry to disappoint you, sista, but you'd be very surprised to learn that African-Americans aren't the only people to suffer racial injustices at the hands of the white man. In fact, our ancestry is quite similar. Slavery dominated not only in America but my ancestors were also brought here from Africa, and they were sold on the markets to slave masters just as yours were. In this part of town, we've always been considered the lower class or minority in the eyes of the more well-to-do French elite."

Yasmina was swamped with guilt. She'd been ridiculing Giddeon in one way or another since first meeting him and she truthfully never could find one fault.

"Look, Giddeon, I'm sorry. I didn't mean for it to sound like. . ."

Giddeon knew the comment was made out of ignorance so it didn't bother him. He'd lived it and knew the only way to make things easier was by working hard.

Waving a hand he said, "Don't mention it. My only concern is helping you blend in and find safety. The only way to achieve this is for you to mingle with people. It's the reason I brought you here."

Yasmina eyed the many dilapidated buildings again, all of them reminding her of remnants of something she'd seen in other places.

"This area is known as Nine-Tres," Giddeon said proudly. "Yes," he continued, "this place is as dangerous as any you've seen : murder, drugs, robbery, it all happens here."

Yasmina wondered why Giddeon elected to put her in areas that were full of poverty and crime. Her question was answered when he said, "I'm not going to pretend like I don't know about your life or situation. When Damita asked for my help, I needed to assure myself that I wasn't getting into something I would regret later. So, I used my investigative skills and searched the Internet and would you believe, your-- "

"My entire life's history came up!" Yasmina yelled. Both of them started laughing.

"And like I was saying before I was rudely interrupted; I know you're used to living in five-star hotels, eating caviar and driving fancy cars, but in order for me to do my part and help you make it from point 'A' to point 'B' safely, bringing you to the 'hood was the best option." Yasmina wrinkled her face and was about to protest when Giddeon added, "Besides, the second you try and order caviar from your penthouse suite, room service will get one look at your pretty face and before you know it, you'll be back in prison eating powdered eggs and drinking spoiled milk."

It was hard to hide the smile, so Yasmina didn't try. "Well, for one, Mr. Private Investigator," Giddeon put a hand over his heart and smiled sarcastically. Yasmina continued. "I don't eat those stinky fish eggs. The stuff is too gross. Secondly, I really do apologize about being so rude and inconsiderate to you. I mean, I can't begin to tell you how grateful I am for all that you've done."

Yasmina walked around the car until her face was inches away from Giddeon's.

"Now, to clear a few things up, I can honestly empathize with you when you speak about your ancestors but I beg to differ on some of the things you said."

Giddeon was confused.

"Well, you see, my ancestors are Jamaican. We speak Patois. I am Jamaican also. So, next time you decide to do research on me, make sure you have your facts straight. Wha' ya say 'bout dat, rude boy!" Yasmina laughed as she spoke in her native tongue. After the two shared a laugh that broke the tension, they conversed all the way to into the building.

CHAPTER FIFTEEN

A Few Days Later

"Brandon!" Serosa yelled, not taking her eyes off of the strange woman. The woman wore dark shades. Her body was partially concealed as she stood behind racks of clothing. Serosa nudged Brandon's arm.

"What?"

"Do you see how that lady keeps staring at me?"

Half-paying any attention to the questions being asked, Brandon shrugged his shoulders. "Nah, what lady?"

The fact of the matter was his interest was on something more appealing, Serosa. She easily slid her curvy body into a Prada dress that bared her shoulders and showed much cleavage, causing him to instantly get hard. They were in the shopping district, minutes away from the Eiffel Tower and across from the River La Seine. After the minor mishap at the hotel they'd previously stayed in, Shotty Dread got them another luxurious suite at Hotel George IV. The street, Avenue Montague, was lined with high-end stores - Dior, Versace, Gucci, Cartier, Prada, Chanel.

As Serosa pranced back and forth in the dressing room mirror, she couldn't get the lady from her mind.

"I've never seen anything so beautiful," she said to herself, admiring the stilettos that matched the outfit.

"Me either," Brandon mumbled as he moved against her body. "And I'll tell you this much," he ran his hands across the silk fabric, her nipples hardening at the touch of his fingers. "I dig the idea of watching us make love in front of a mirror this size."

"Boy, stop it!" Serosa smacked Brandon's hands lightly. "I was talkin' about the dress, stupid."

Although she was joking, she knew Brandon was dead serious. He suddenly got quiet, the only noise being heard was the rustling of fabric as he kneaded her breasts and begin to grind against her round ass.

"And I was talkin' 'bout us," he countered as he started kissing the nape of her neck.

Serosa suppressed a moan that came from deep within. Brandon pulled his hard dick out and drove her crazy as it moved in between the folds of her buttocks. With each thrust the flimsy material wedged deeper until she could almost feel penetration in her vagina.

She arched her back. He dug deeper. He was now under the dress, his fingers invading her wet pussy. Serosa's warm juices ran down her thighs and she cried out as Brandon entered her from behind. He pulled her thong to the side. With her palms spread flat across the glass, she watched as Brandon stroked her, his body trembling slightly each time she gyrated her hips. For what seem like an hour, but what was really only minutes, Brandon stroked her sweet pussy, covering her mouth to muffle her moans. When they finished the smell of sex filled the small room, finger prints were smeared on the mirror. Both of them released tension that managed to build up over the past few days.

Brandon stared at Serosa as she changed back into her clothing. What he saw amazed him. Serosa wasn't the same shy girl who pushed away from his advances or lacked confidence in her own body. When he first met her, she barely knew how to French kiss. She still had that innocence of a virgin. Now he saw someone entirely different. She was naughty, racy and uninhibited when it came to sex, and he loved it. Soon afterwards they were back at the hotel. Again, Serosa stood by a mirror as she undressed.

"Baby, there's something different about you," Brandon said, eyeing Serosa from afar. He moved in to investigate.

"Different, what do you mean, different?"

Brandon only stared. At one point he touched her butt then her stomach. "I, I don't know. Maybe I'm trippin'. It's nothing, don't worry about it."

Truth of the mtatter was Brandon didn't want to tell Serosa she was putting on weight. Instead of confrontations with such a comment, he decided to drop it and started flipping through channels on the t.v.

"Owww! Whatcha do that for?" Brandon held the back of his head with a hand. Serosa had abruptly smacked him.

"How are you just gonna come off and tell me that I'm getting fat, then try to avoid talking about it like it was nothing?" She stood over him fuming.
Her hands were on her hips as she awaited an answer.

"Girl, you trippin'." Brandon tried laughing it off, but deep inside he'd noticed the mood swings, figuring it to be stress because of the situation they were in.

Not receiving the response she was looking for, Serosa stormed into the bathroom, slamming the door behind her. Unbeknownst to Serosa and Brandon, the drug the President created, Cephzysin-07N, was having an effect.

CHAPTER SIXTEEN

FORSYTH COUNTY JAIL
1 Month Prior

Shukre was pissed when the c.o. beckoned him; he was in the middle of a heated discussion as he battled another inmate in a game of chess.

You expect me to believe that you and - what cha say yo' man's name is?"

"Dalvin," Shukre mumbled.

"Yeah, yo' man, Dalvin," the inmate, Dirty, repeated. "He broke into a fucking federal penitentiary, one with gun towers and state of the art computer equipment that could track a rat fucking, and the two of you helped some chick on death row escape a few days before her execution was set to take place?"

Noticing the bewildered expression on Dirty's face, Shukre yelled, "Damn, son, you don't believe I'm capable of pulling something like that off?"

Dirty chuckled. His next move was a castle.

When Shukre realized he wasn't convincing enough, his agitation grew.

"Gimmie dat knight, nigga!" he huffed, grabbing the ceramic horse off the cardboard. "How you gon' let me come into your house like that? It's the same strategy used the night of the prison break."

Dirty was pissed, he didn't like the way Shukre ridiculed him. The last person who tried to play him paid a severe penalty. Dirty remained quiet and took the insults as he was mentally contemplating his next move. Dirty put his index finger and thumb on his rook, stationing the ceramic piece until it aligned vertically with Shukre's knight. He eyed Shukre.

"I expect you to make a calculated and well-thought-out decision before you decide to go any further, brotha." He paused for seconds before adding, "If you expect me to believe half of what you say, then show me what you got, homie."

Shukre studied the board. His concentration was on sealing the deal, not giving his opponent another chance but Dirty's continuous taunts almost made concentrating impossible.

"Nigga tryna tell me he pulled something like that off," Dirty ranted. "What kinda fool you take me for? You must think I got locked up yesterday." Chuckling, Dirty added, "Nigga, I've run across jokers like you all my life. Once they get locked up they become all sorts of actors, rappers, R&B singers. Hell, I've even heard a few of them claim to be best-selling authors."

Dirty paused momentarily, feeling he'd succeeded in annoying Shukre.

"But yo, I gots to admit, homie, you got me when you claimed to break someone out of a maximum security prison. That's some Jack-Bauer-24 shit for real." Wrinkling his brow he asked, "What did you say you were in her for, simple possession of marijuana?"

The insult sliced through Shukre like a Ginsu knife. Shukre, not happy in the least bit, shot Dirty a look that could kill. But, he also realized that someone as stubborn and pigheaded as Dirty wasn't going to be easily convinced. What he really needed was proof.

Still seated around the table, Shukre told stories about Yasmina, things he'd heard from Dalvin. In detail, he recited the incident during the bike rally in Myrtle Beach. He even spoke about the amount of drugs Yasmina pushed on the streets of Winston-Salem. It wasn't until Shukre went into the episode that happened inside Yasmina's prison cell that Dirty's expression changed to one of interest.

"Damn, dawg!" Dirty said. "Yo girl Yasmina's one cold bitch. You mean she ripped the guard's boxers?"

"Hold up," Shukre interrupted, "I ain't near finished yet." He was glad to have finally won Dirty's approval. "Anyways, this crazy bitch removes a jar of Vaseline from a table, puts a huge glob between her fingers, slaps it between the guard's butt cheeks and grabs his nightstick."

Just then, a commotion from the t.v. room interrupted Shukre. Glancing in that direction, he noticed a lot of inmates pointing and gawking at something on the news.

"Hold tight, dawg, I'll be back," Shukre said as he walked over to the crowd. When his eyes registered on what was airing, he yelled, "Ay, Dirt, come 'ere!" waving his arms furiously while his eyes stayed glued to the television.

Dirty couldn't believe what he was seeing, his mouth fell open. What he saw before him, was a picture of

Yasmina and a news reporter telling about the daring escape as she stood just outside the severed fence of USP Carrollton.

"Thought I was lying, huh?" Shukre smiled. "I told you, man, I run with people that's connected, dawg."

They made their way back over to the table where they were playing chess. With his hand hovering over the board, Shukre took his next move.

"Checkmate, nigga!"

Dirty smiled, though behind the fake sneer was malice. He knew he couldn't beat Shukre in the game of chess. The entire time they played, he cheated when Shukre wasn't paying attention. But the game of life was a different story and he'd been in jail enough times to know when a get-out-of-jail-free-card was right in his face.

Casually, Dirty stood to his feet.

"Man, man," he said, eyeing Shukre. "At first I had my doubts about you, but you've proven yourself worthy." Leaning in closer, his mouth merely inches away form Shukre's nose, Dirty said, "You got me. You beat me in the game of chess, but, let's see how you do when it comes to your life." He walked off heading for the officers' station, leaving Shukre with a puzzled look on his face.

CHAPTER SEVENTEEN

PARIS, FRANCE

Darkness slowly descended upon the city. The breathtaking beauty stretching as far as the eyes could see couldn't shake the sadness that consumed Yasmina.

For the first time in ten years she finally had the opportunity to walk the aisles of stores and shop for finer things that were in her life at one time or another - Gucci, Prada, Fendi, Cartier, Chanel and other high-end designers. Yasmina was happy again for the moment. She felt renewed as she tried on garment after garment. After a while, she found herself parading in front of the mirror. Yasmina's quest for newness didn't stop with clothing; that was a material need. She wanted something that would last, something no one could take away from her. She wanted a makeover, a person she could glance in the mirror at on any given day and be proud of, not someone who had to remember the pain and suffering inflicted upon her by men who violated her body. It's the reason that days before, Giddeon had taken her to a chapel where she could have a one-on-one with God.

Despite all of the making over, ridding herself of the old and welcoming in the new, there was still a piece of Yasmina missing. As she watched people roam the streets of Clinchy, she couldn't help wondering about Serosa.

Something told her that the girl in the boutique earlier was Serosa. She leaned against the railing on the balcony, her mind overwhelmed with thoughts of her daughter. Giddeon, not wanting to interrupt her thoughts, said nothing as he focused on the deep yearning in her eyes. Seconds passed before he said, "You know, I don't doubt what you're saying. Only the love of a parent could discern when something isn't right about a child." His pause caused her to turn her head in his direction. "But why here, I mean, of all the places she could have come to in Paris, why would Shotty Dread bring her to Clinchy?"

Yasmina's posture wavered. It was the very same question she'd asked herself all day long, but she wasn't sure of the answer. Tears started running down her face. Giddeon noticed this. He then noticed her legs buckle. Walking behind her, he gently placed a hand on Yasmina's shoulder. His touch startled her and she tried stifling the sobs but they kept coming.

With his right hand clutching her elbow, Giddeon spun Yasmina around, their eyes locking. As hard as he tried not to stare, he couldn't shake her gaze. Yasmina's lips, the shiny gloss making them full and sexy, made his dick rock hard.

As he searched for the words to say, his eyes wandered down her body and locked on her cleavage. Giddeon trembled. His manhood throbbed, his heart was pounding. Although Giddeon knew what he was feeling at this exact moment was a shared attraction, he could sense the rigidness of Yasmina's body as she stood before him.

When Giddeon moved his head closer, Yasmina parted her lips. For seconds he took in her tongue, the intensity was unbearable. Yasmina fought desperately to stop the throbbing between her legs; it was a heat and moistness she hadn't felt since Scorcher.

With her head tilted back, Yasmina guided Giddeon's mouth around her nipple. The moment his warm lips enveloped her swollen nipples, she moaned. Giddeon's hands were busy caressing her clit, their one time strictly business association was no more. They'd crossed the line. It wasn't long before Yasmina's dress fell to the floor. She didn't bother crossing her arms in from of her breasts; this wasn't prison.

Giddeon attacked Yasmina's body. The long kisses on her neck sent chills down her spine. Yasmina was lost in the bliss of what she was feeling. She hadn't felt like this in the last ten years. Giddeon took her face into his hands. He nibbled her tongue, his head moved to her wet pussy. Yasmina fought the urge to cry out. She danced on her toes, her legs unstable as sensation of Giddeon's tongue licking her sweet juices sent her over the edge. They finished what they started on the balcony inside the room.

Awaking early the next morning, Giddeon was surprised to find Yasmina still in a deep slumber, her head nestled snugly against his chest, her body resting on his. There was the pleasant smell of fresh brewed coffee wafting inside the kitchenette when Yasmina finally stepped through the door. She wore only a shirt, a white button-down Giddeon had on the night before, and a pair of panties.

With a sheepish grin on her face, she sipped the hot cup of coffee Giddeon handed her.

"I see Sleeping Beauty has finally awakened," he smiled. He leaned in pecking Yasmina on the lips.

Yasmina didn't fight it or turn her head away. She sat with her legs folded beneath her. Yet there was something that nagged Yasmin and before she could go any further with her feelings, the questions had to be asked. Sliding the cup away from her body, she leaned on both elbows.

"Giddeon," she said, getting his full attention. "There's something I have to ask you, a two-part question, and if you feel as though the question deserves an answer, I would like to hear it. But," she gestured both hands in the air, "if you don't answer, that's cool also."

The comment caught Giddeon by surprise. He sat next to her.

"What is it?" he asked, although he felt he already knew where Yasmina was heading.

"Well," she started, her smile turning serious, "earlier you said you'd run a check on me to determine if you should involve yourself in my situation. Do you regret it?"

Giddeon opened his mouth but was interrupted when Yasmina said, “Hold up, I told you it was a two-part question.”

The last question caused Giddeon to get up from the table. Walking over to the window, he stared into the distance filled with confusion. He never got the chance to answer as the cell phone started ringing.

CHAPTER EIGHTEEN

PORTLAND, OREGON

Damita had just placed the phone on the base when a knock came at her door. She wanted an update on Yasmina's situation so she called the number Giddeon had given her.

She was a prisoner in her own home as she began being interrogated by the same agent who'd been shot and left for dead. She was fast becoming irritated by the man's accusations.

"Mrs. DeMarcus," Chief Sculea exclaimed, his tone somewhat harsh. "You expect me to believe you had nothing to do with this?"

Damita sat back in the recliner. For days, she'd been getting visits from one police officer after another. She knew they were trying to work an angle that would tie her to the people responsible for killing the agent. Damita maintained her composure. "Honestly, Agent - what's your name again?" she asked in a tone that conveyed her disgust.

"Chief, Chief Sculea," he stated matter of factly.

"Well, *Chief* Sculea," Damita repeated, "like I was saying, as far as I'm concerned, you're going to believe what you want to. If I tell you the truth you'll say I'm lying. If I lie, you won't believe it either. What's left for me to say?"

The anger on the Chief's face was discernible for miles. He moved so that he was now towering over Damita.

"I just can't believe you expect me to buy that you had no idea what was taking place inside your own home. I mean, how is it that three armed men, one of them a fugitive, casually walked into your living room and abducted an eighteen-year-old girl who was supposed to be under your supervision?"

Damita rolled her eyes at him.

"In case you didn't know, I'm an entrepreneur; I have three businesses in other states. I have hair shows booked overseas, and I'm in and out the country for days or weeks at a time." After pausing and letting the words sink in, Damita added, "So, you're the policeman. . ."

"Federal Agent," countered the Chief.

"Oh, excuse me!" Damita sarcastically spat. "Mr. police-federal-agent man, *you* tell *me* how it is that you let some maniac killer just walk into my home and kidnap Serosa and your agency didn't even put an Amber Alert in the news?"

Chief Sculea was at a loss for words.

"That's what I thought!" Damita yelled. "If you're done badgering me about something I don't know and have nothing to do with, I think I'll go to the media myself with the story. Maybe they'll do some real investigating into what happened, unlike you policeman who wear uniforms just for show."

The comment stung. Chief Sculea knew Damita had a point. He tried smoothing over the situation.

"Look, Mrs. DeMarcus, the media isn't privy to every piece of information that we have. When the story first broke of the escapee, we only knew he was spotted in this area. I had no idea he was targeting your home until we learned that he had a past with Yasmina."

"You're saying he kidnapped Serosa in order to get to Yasmina?"

Although Damita already knew this, the shock on her face registered something different. "Is that what you're telling me, Chief? So, you were using Serosa as bait, is that it?"

The Chief now stood near the spot where his partner, Agent Wallace, died. "I'm not comfortable making these accusations Mrs. DeMarcus, but I lost my partner here. He was a good man." After clearing his throat, he uttered, "If I hadn't have been wearing my vest, I would've been dead also. So, you have to understand, when I'm questioning you, it's not to make you a suspect or to try and implicate you. I'm only following leads hoping something or someone can shed light on the situation, and maybe we can apprehend this guy. Can you understand my frustration?"

"No!" Damita answered rather quickly.

Her response puzzled the Chief.

"Believe me when I say this, I'm sorry for your loss, but I'm a victim in all of this too. I've lost somebody. Serosa's human also, but I haven't heard you mention or apologize for her abduction. What about my home?" Damita continued. "It was invaded by some murderer. What about me? I could've been lying dead right beside your partner. You were there when the men did what they did. You saw when they threatened my life also. Did you ever take a second to think about that?"

Chief Sculea was stumped. Clearing away the lump that started to rise in his throat he uttered, “Mrs. DeMarcus, I owe you an apology. I’m sorry.”

He was about to continue when his cell phone rang.

“Call me if you can think of anything,” he mouthed to Damita walking out the door.

Not a second after the door closed, Damita’s home phone rang.

“Hello?” She answered.

“We have to talk,” the caller stated, hanging up soon after.

CHAPTER NINETEEN

Attorney Standridge was furious. He strummed his fingers against the steering wheel as he drove. The past few weeks had been stressful. First, there was the laborious motion for a stay of execution he fought for on behalf of his client, Yasmina, one the district court judge opposed at a time seemingly critical. Then there was the prison break.

The attorney was in the middle of a conference call when the jaw-dropping news broke. Unbeknownst to him and the gentlemen seated around the table, their meeting had to take a back seat when his secretary, Shelly, poked her head inside the room.

"Uh, Mr. Standridge, sir," she said popping gum between her sentences. "You have a call on line 1."

Shelly was barely 5-feet-tall but wore a pair of four-inch pumps. Her sandy-blonde hair made her resemble a cross between Sharon Stone and Mel Gibson. And though she was unprofessional in every sense of the word, Attorney Standridge couldn't fire his niece.

Shelly waited at the door, her fingers pelting away at the glass as she waited for a response. The expression on Attorney Standridge's face clearly showed how annoyed he was. He was in talks with two prominent attorneys from another law firm, trying to find a way to reverse the decision made by the judge so that they could come up with a better defense for Yasmina.

Letting out a deep sigh, he dropped his pen to the table. "Shelly, I thought I told you to hold all calls. I'm in an important meeting. "

"Uncle," she slipped catching herself by placing a hand to her mouth then smirking, "I mean, Mr. Standridge, you might want to take this call."

The two other gentlemen, Harold Mundy and Thomas Diane, of the firm Daine, Mundy, Mundy & Associates, glanced at each other.

"Did the caller mention what it pertained to?" asked Attorney Standridge.

He couldn't believe the audacity of his niece. There weren't many opportunities for private attorneys to impress people with the credentials of Mundy and Daine. They were top notch. The crème–de- la-crème when it came to cases like the one he was fighting an uphill battle to win.

Attorneys like Mundy and Daine were on another level, a plane he hoped to get to. The two were top dogs when it came to overturned convictions and between both of them, they had netted three-hundred-twenty overturned cases in their thirty-one years working in law.

In the back of Attorney Standridge's mind, he almost knew what the call was about. During a visit with Yasmina before the escape, she told some disturbing stories of what had been happening to her while in prison. After taking these accusations to the warden, along with threats of a lawsuit and leaking the information to the media, the warden assured him that he'd call with a solution to the problem. When Shelly said, "It's the warden of USP Carrolton calling to inform you that your client, Yasmina, escaped early this morning," Attorney Standridge's face lost all color.

Now, as his mind raced back to that day in the office weeks ago, he whacked the steering wheel with his fist. Seconds later he pulled into Damita's driveway.

"I promise you," Damita protested, "I had nothing to do with it. I didn't have the slightest idea that Yasmina was planning to escape."

The attorney eyed Damita. "Mrs. DeMarcus, please forgive me for saying so, but that's quite hard to believe." For seconds they stared at each other.

"Put yourself in my shoes. I'm a defense attorney representing a client you hired for me. All of a sudden she escapes, vanishes into thin air, and you expect me to believe you don't know anything about it?"

Attorney Standridge slowly moved around Damita. They were situated in the den, just beyond the fireplace. He continued.

"Can you imagine how embarrassed I was when the Feds stormed into my office accusing me of aiding in the escape of a prisoner? Not to mention the fact that I hired two of the most prestigious attorneys to help me on this case. You can bet that our chances of winning this case are slim-to-none."

Damita remained silent, deep in thought.

"Honestly, sir, I'm very sorry about everything you've been through. It's been weeks since Yasmina escaped and if I'm correct, three weeks ago to this day she would've been put to death. You said so yourself when you informed me that the judge was upholding the motion you appealed."

The attorney was speechless. He knew everything Damita said was true, but it didn't justify what happened. He found his voice.

"Mrs. DeMarcus, in my line of work I've seen cases overturned at the last minute that prosecutors thought were already decided by landslide margins. I know that you may view the way we handle cases as gambling with your friend's life, but believe me when I say I think we've got something, or we did have something that possibly would've gotten Yasmina off."

For a quick moment Damita's heart fluttered with joy, but it soon passed.

"I've been questioned by the Feds almost everyday since the news broke," she said, removing any suspicion about her role in the escape. "Not even fifteen minutes ago, when you called, they were here."

"What did you tell them?"

"What could I tell them?" Damita yelled. "Like I've told them everyday, they think they already know all the answers so why bother asking me?" Damita was by the fireplace.

"I've told them about being accosted in my own home at gunpoint by three armed men, the same men who kidnapped Serosa, Yasmina's daughter."

"Hold on!" Attorney Standridge interrupted. "You mean to tell me someone came in and kidnapped Serosa?" Damita nodded her head. He continued. "I didn't hear mention of this on the news, why didn't they air that and why didn't you call me?"

Attorney Standridge rested his elbow against the mantel of the fireplace. He was in deep thought. Staring down into the burning wood, he tried piecing things together but nothing made sense. Just as he opened his mouth to speak, the front door swung open.

CHAPTER TWENTY

No badges were flashed, no introductions given. The strange men only stared at Damita and the attorney as they inched closer to the fireplace.

The two men had been waiting for hours. They'd patiently watched and waited for the agents who entered Damita's home earlier, to leave. As they'd eyed Chief Sculea backing out of the driveway, they knew time was of the essence.

"Whatcha' think?" the taller asked his partner.

"I don't think there's anything we can use," the shorter gentleman replied, gripping the steering wheel until his knuckles turned white.

Placing the listening device back inside its case, the shorter of the two sighed. "I still can't make the connection between Yasmina and the guy who escaped from prison. We need to find Dalvin; he will be the answer to all of our questions."

"What if they are working together?" he shot a quick glance at his partner. "I mean, they both are Jamaican, both had death sentences looming over their heads and it's not just a coincidence that both somehow managed to escape from prison weeks apart. If you ask me, they've been planning this from the beginning."

A confused expression came over the shorter man's face. "You think this Dalvin guy could be the piece that links this puzzle together?" he asked, realizing where his partner was heading.

"That, and the DeMarcus woman. There's a connection; she has knowledge of it but somehow she's able to deceive the Feds."

Grabbing the door handle, the shorter man said, "Let's get the information we need."

At first glance, Damita thought the men were agents. "Look," she sighed, her hands on her hips, "I've had a long day and answered enough of your questions. Can you guys come back tomorrow? Better yet, I'll come to your office tomorrow."

The taller man looked uneasy, he ruffled his jacket. Both wore dark suits, their shirts were unfastened at the top. When one of the men reached inside his coat the handle of a gun came into view. Both Damita and the attorney gasped.

"My name's Agent Simms," the shorter man produced a leather wallet, quickly flashing his credentials. He looked to his partner, "Agent Pratt."

Damita heaved a long sigh of relief. She didn't know what to make of the men when they first entered her home but after seeing the badges, she relaxed a little.

"Well," she said moving near a chair, "like I said before, if you gentlemen wouldn't mind, I'd appreciate it if you let me stop by tomorrow. I have company."

"That won't be necessary, Mrs. DeMarcus," interrupted Agent Pratt. "We have only a few questions for you and we'll gladly be on our way."

Attorney Standridge's shifted in his chair. There was something about the men that worried him. He wasn't certain of their claims and even more disturbing, he felt

Damita was oblivious to the performance. In his twenty-two years of working in the judicial system, he'd never crossed paths with two more suspicious individuals than the ones standing in front of him.

"I 'm sorry, what agency did you say you represented?"

Agent Pratt immediately whipped out his gun.

Damita's eyes grew large as fear snaked through her body.

Agent Pratt interjected, "I see this won't be easy as we thought." He eyed Agent Simms, who removed clear plastic trash bag ties from his jacket pocket. Agent Pratt roughly grabbed Damita by the hair, slinging her against the wall. Attorney Standridge just stood there, helpless, with the cold barrel of Agent Simm's .9 mm at his head.

"You can make this easy, or you can make this ugly," Agent Pratt threatened. The questions I ask are simple and I'll only ask once."

The situation was bad. Attorney Standridge knew from the frightened look on Damita's face that she would crack under pressure. His eyes flickered toward the fireplace.

There, resting in a brass rack sitting at the far end beside a small stack of wood were two solid steel rods - fire pokers.

Agent Pratt continued his inquiry. "Now that we've established what's important, let's talk about a person of interest."

Damita searched her memory bank but could come up with nothing. She could see the malicious intent in the man's eyes and knew before long he would carry through with his threat of violence.

"I, I'm not certain that I know anyone by that name," she answered, her voice quivering with each word.

Casually taking a puff of his cigarette and exhaling a huge plume of smoke from his lungs, Agent Pratt gave a nod to his partner. Attorney Standridge suddenly let out a bloodcurdling scream as his pinky finger snapped like twig. Damita cried out, "Please, I'm being honest; I don't know anyone by the name of Shukre Herring!"

Agent Pratt started choking Damita. He shoved the barrel of his gun in her mouth.

"So you're willing to let whoever this man is die so you can keep your co-conspirators safe? Is that it?" he spoke through clenched teeth.

Damita couldn't speak, her mouth was numb. She shook her head. "No!"

Agent Pratt continued, "You mean to tell me you don't even know the man who helped your cousin, Dalvin, break Yasmina out of prison?"

Damita and the attorney locked eyes.

Agent Pratt noticed their connection. "So," he nodded at the attorney, "you didn't know that your little friend here was the one who orchestrated the entire escape?"

"Wow, no." Attorney Standridge sighed, shocked by this information.

"Well, sorry for ruining your secret, but how do you think we found out about you and what you did?" the agent said to Damita. Not giving her enough time to respond he said, "Shukre spilled; he told everything he knew. We know it was you who planned and funded the operation and it was your cousin, Dalvin, who pulled the act off."

Even though the attorney suffered from excruciating pain, he mustered enough strength to shoot Damita another glance.

"That's cool, don't answer me," Agent Pratt chided screwing the silencer onto the end of his gun. "I have ways of getting the information I want."

Just as he aimed his gun at Damita's head, there was a knock at the door. "Go check on that," he instructed his partner.

Dalvin had been listening in on the exchange for quite some time. When he first arrived on Damita's street, he noticed something strange - a beige sedan sat parked in the center of the driveway.

This ain't right, he thought as he parked his rental a couple houses away. For minutes he watched the two men get out of the car and slowly made their way to the front door. When the taller man, Agent Simms reached into his pocket and retrieved what appeared to be a silencer, screwing it on his gun as he cautiously moved near the front door, Dalvin decided at that moment to investigate. As the two men entered the house, shouldering the door and making a quick entrance, thoughts of what Dalvin learned about Shukre and his entire family crossed his mind.

Damita's in danger! The thought tugged at his heart. For a while, he didn't want to believe it was true, Shukre and his family dying horrible and violent deaths. The flight had taken him almost four hours, changing planes at two different locations. But after stopping by a storage unit not too far away from where Damita lived, he was now glad he'd gotten what he needed.

Dalvin could hear footsteps as they came closer. In the living room there weren't many places to hide. The only thing spacious enough was a tall wooden grandfather clock. It protruded from the corner enough for Dalvin to squeeze behind it.

Now, as he made himself as small as he could, there was another problem. Dalvin shook his head from side to side as he farted. The sounds were low, but were still obvious.

Why the fuck does this have to happen, he cursed to himself.

Dalvin watched the man stop in mid-stride. He turned on his heels as the sounds emitting from behind the clock grew louder.

Shit! Dalvin grimaced, his heart beating fast. *This muthafucka did hear me fart. Damn!*

The man was no more than ten steps away. Dalvin, not wanting to expose himself, didn't peek around the clock. When his eyes caught what appeared to be an extended arm holding a .9 mm with a black silencer screwed to it slowly inching towards him, he did what came to mind.

The blow caused a muffled sound near Dalvin's ear. The bullet lodged into the wall inches away from his head. Another bullet ricocheted off the clock. Dalvin and the man struggled, wrestling for the gun clenched tightly in the agent's hand. When he couldn't think of any other way to release the gun form the man's strong grip, Dalvin shoved his knee into the agent's groin.

"Hey, Simms!" Agent Pratt yelled.

There's that voice again, Dalvin thought as he realized he was fast running out of time. He knew if the other man made it into the room, everyone, including himself, would be dead. With a powerful lunge, Dalvin chopped downward with the weapon he'd retrieved from storage -a .25 automatic Damita refused to keep in her house. The tall man, Agent Simms, collapsed on the floor, the gun still gripped in his hand.

Agent Pratt's eyes grew large the moment he rounded the corner. His partner was a crumpled heap, his body sprawled over the floor. But it was Agent's Pratt own nonchalant attitude that caused him to become an added fixture to the floor, beside his partner. His arrogance didn't allow him to see the vicious blow coming toward his head as Dalvin caught him directly on the temple.

CHAPTER TWENTY-ONE

"Oh yeah!" Dalvin smirked, surprised at the stubbornness Agent Pratt possessed. It had been almost fifteen minutes of smacks, punches and threats and the man still wouldn't relinquish any information. "Well," Dalvin stated, shaking his head continuously, "before this is over, you'll be willing to tell me everything I wanna know!"

Dalvin's finality didn't faze the agent. He'd been trained for this type of encounter and knew there was no way he could be forced to divulge anything, even if it meant death. He was bound with duct tape while his wrist, ankles, and feet were tied to a chair. Though his mouth was partially crammed with a cloth, Agent Pratt still managed to utter arrogant remarks.

Dalvin took the insults in stride. A time or two, he glanced in the direction of Agent Simms who unconsciously snored, a sure sign that the lick he'd taken to the head had had quite an impact. A purple lump the size of a golf ball bulged from his head.

For moments, both Damita and Attorney Standridge, who hadn't spoken word one about what was happening, stared at Dalvin. He moved like a man with purpose.

When Dalvin returned from the garage where three of Damita's cars sat parked, his hands were full. "What are you going to do with that?" asked the attorney. He held a bewildered expression as Dalvin clamped a small battery pack to the bottom of a drill and pressed a trigger. The drill roared to life.

The screech the machine made caused both Damita and the attorney to step back. Their eyes met then fell on Dalvin's.

"Go in the kitchen," he eyed Damita, ignoring the question the attorney had asked him. "Take a bowl out, fill it half with water and the other half baby oil. Put it in the microwave until I tell you to take it out."

Damita questioned his instructions. She knew when he set out to do something, he would go all the way with it.

After fastening a six-inch screw to the end of the drill, Dalvin smiled.

"Yeah, muthafucka, I bet when I finish with yo' ass, you'll whistle Dixie if I ask you to."

He had an evil grin that scared the attorney shitless. "Now, son," Attorney Standridge attempted, "don't you think we should let the law handle this? I mean, you can't just take matters into your own hands; that's called vigilante justice."

Dalvin's eyes cut to the attorney. "Look here, you old bastard, if it weren't for me, yo' ass would've been dead and stankin' right here in this house. When the *law*," he teased emphasizing the word, "finally would've found you, the maggots would've had your body so eaten up, the only way they would've identified yo' fat ass was by your dental records.

These two bitches killed my boy. They made calls to my house and if they would've caught me or my family there, I wouldn't have lived to save yo' fat ass. So, while you're so caught up on wantin' me to let the law handle it, you need to be thanking me for saving your life."

Sweat seeped into the attorney's eyes. He knew Dalvin was right but he'd taken a sworn oath to abide by the law of the land. He was about to speak when Dalvin interrupted.

"Never mind though!" he met Damita as she walked through the door. "Once I'm finished with this piece of shit, if he lives, you can let the law handle it then. For now, I'ma' find out who they work for, and what's really going on."

Agent Pratt nervously looked at Attorney Standridge, his eyes showing fear for the first time. Watching this madman in front of him holding a drill in his hands and directing Damita to heat up a bowl of baby oil made the agent second-guess his decision not to talk. He was too late as Dalvin walked in the direction of his partner, Agent Simms, and doused a quarter of the hot liquid into his face.

The piercing yelp was drowned as Dalvin instructed Damita to raise the volume on the sound system. Agent Simms grabbed his face and thrashed around on the floor. Attorney Standridge vomited after he looked at the melted skin sticking to the agent's fingers.

Agent Pratt fumed, he jerked as he struggled to free himself. Veins protruded on his forehead as his anger grew. It didn't help any when Dalvin laughed at the agent floundering around the room like a fish out of water. Dalvin wasn't done.

Looking at Damita he said, "You think he's gon' be any trouble?"

Damita's eyes slowly panned toward the attorney, who screamed, "No, no problem at all!"

Smirking, Dalvin hissed, "Yeah, I figured yo' bitch ass would say something like that. Bring yo' fat ass over here!"

Attorney Standridge moved like he had a twenty-pound bowling ball attached to his feet. His posture no longer held that regal air about it; he slumped as he walked.

For seconds, the attorney avoided grabbing hold of the drill. Each time Dalvin pressed it into his hands, he would release his grip.

"Look here, ol' man!" Dalvin squared up until his nose was pressed against Attorney Standridge's. "If I have to shoot you in the ass to make you see that I ain't got time for no bullshit, I'll do it. Now, hold this muthafucka tight and don't let it go."

The attorney was traumatized. He couldn't shake the sight of the man on the floor. The things Dalvin had done to him. His eyes were melted shut.

XXXXXXXX

The dream was one Damita hadn't had in a long time - at least the last ten years. She could remember it like it happened yesterday. They were in the hotel room in Myrtle Beach.

"No! No!" Scorcher yelled, pleading at the top of his lungs. He'd just been insulted and humiliated having been forced to have sex with his best friend, Hassan, at the hands of four females. His ego was already shattered but when he realized that the women weren't quite finished, he pleaded for his life.

"Please!" he cried out, tears streaming down his face. "You don't have to kill us, I'm embarrassed enough as it is. Please, I'll get you your money."

Damita came back to reality and covered her ears after Agent Pratt started screaming.

"Please!" he begged as Dalvin forced the attorney to drill a hole deep into his knee cap. "Shit, please!" he cried. "I'll tell you what it is you want to know. No more, please, no more!"

Dalvin was impressed. After drilling holes through each of Agent's Pratt's hands, he thought the man would tell even his darkest secrets, but he didn't. It wasn't until

Attorney Standridge made it to the second knee cap and Dalvin warned that each of his toes would be next, did Agent Pratt talk.

Looking at the attorney, Dalvin said, "You know what, ol' man, you impressed me. I ain't think you had it in you." Prying the drill from the dazed attorney's hands, Dalvin gently patted his shoulder. "Even though I think you got a bit carried away, I ain't tell you to get all ghetto on that muthafucka. I mean, you went to work when you took it upon yo'self to go at my man's knee caps; that shit surprised me."

When Dalvin had finally almost run out of words, he said, "Now, you may think I'm wrong for forcing you to take part in this shit but we received the information we were looking for. The information surprised the fuck out of you and I couldn't let you get any bright ideas to take me or my cousin, Damita, to the cops." After a slight pause he finished. "Last question: Knowing these two muthafuckas was gon' kill yo' ass, do you feel sorry about doing what 'cha did?"

Attorney Standridge stumbled over to the nearest chair and plopped in it. He was too dazed to respond.

CHAPTER TWENTY-TWO

"How could this be?" Attorney Standridge stammered. He was still somewhat in denial at the astonishing news he heard earlier.

The attorney had gathered his wits. He no longer moped around feeling sorry for himself for the role he played in getting the agent to talk. Standing beside Dalvin and Damita, for seconds he stared at the two men who were now taped to chairs.

"I wonder what else would be revealed about the President if more information fell into the wrong hands? Luckily we're playing on the good side of the law."

Although Dalvin didn't express what he already knew, mainly about people working in government factions, he beamed with delight. *Someone finally saw the trifling shit these muthafuckas do when they work for the government.*

A slight smile appeared on Dalvin's face only to be erased when Attorney Standridge added, "As outrageous as the accusations sound, it's hard to believe that two people, who were questioned in different areas and couldn't hear what the other had said, would concoct the same story if it wasn't true." As his own words sank in, the attorney's hand flew to his mouth like he'd discovered something.

"What is it?" Damita asked, noting his expression.

"Now I get it!" the attorney spoke as if no one else in the room existed.

"What?" Damita questioned again. She was again ignored when the man mumbled to himself.

Fed up, Dalvin approached the attorney, placing a hand on his shoulder. They locked eyes.

"Listen here, you old son-of-a-bitch. You startin' to piss me off with all that mumbling shit. Now, my cousin asked you twice about what it is you think you've found and I wanna hear it."

Dalvin's words quickly got the attorney's attention. "Oh, uh, you see," he stumbled, his delivery coming like a professor in a college giving a dissertation or speech. "The last time I visited with Yasmina, she told me some disturbing news."

Before the attorney could go any farther, both Dalvin and Damita simultaneously interrupted, "What news?"

Attorney Standridge replayed everything Yasmina told him about the rape and the abuse. "When she received the threat from the Senator, who now is the President of the United States, she told the warden of the prison to go forward with the execution."

Dalvin and Damita's responses were the same: their mouth's fell open. Damita's heart ached, she couldn't remove the thought of Yasmina being raped from her head. After all the times she'd visited with her, Yasmina revealed nothing.

"We need to take this to the authorities," Standridge said.

The words hit Dalvin like he'd run into a brick wall. In one quick dash, he was standing before the attorney, his eyes reading murder.

"What 'cha mean, take this to the authorities?"

The attorney watched Dalvin's monstrous fist clench. The tightness across Dalvin's massive hand warned the attorney that he was treading on thin ice.

"Now, now here me out, son," The attorney stammered. After he was sure he had Dalvin's attention he added, "You have to trust me on this one. I know in the beginning I didn't come across as someone who condoned what happened here today but after realizing what you said earlier about these sons'-a-bitches sparing my life, I realize that you were right. As bad as I want them dead, we gotta let justice take its course."

"You gots to be out'cho damn mind if you think I'm gon' let these two bitches walk out of here alive," Dalvin yelled.

"I know you don't approve," the attorney countered, trying to find a solid basis to convince Dalvin of what is morally right, "but trust me, I know people who can and will do what's right in this matter."

Dalvin abruptly whipped out the .9 mm he'd taken off of one of the men. "Yeah, and I know somebody who will do what's right also." Racking the chamber back, he placed the gun to Agent Pratt's head. "I was at the door listening when these slime balls were preparing to kill you and my cousin. Now, I don't know about you, but I've already lost someone dear to me behind this piece of shit sittin' in this chair. If I didn't arrive when I did, my cousin," he pointed at Damita, "would've been next."

Attorney Standridge was at a loss for words. This thing was already out of hand when he took part in torture, but murder!

"Look," interjected the attorney. "If you're worried about these two turning their stories around and denying everything they'd told us, it won't work. They've been traveling across the country on a murder spree. Once a prosecutor gets their testimonies in front of a judge, it's over for them and the President."

Dalvin laughed. He then turned serious.

"You know what, whatever yo' name is? That speech you made probably has won you many cases throughout your years as a lawyer." Dalvin followed by clapping his hands. "But the way I see it, if the President has his hand in on this, there ain't no law, court, or person in their right mind gon' believe anything we have to say, especially after these two let them know I'm the one who helped Yasmina escape."

Attorney Standridge couldn't believe what he was hearing. How could Dalvin go up against someone such as the President? His question was answered when Dalvin said, "And after I get rid of these two bodies, we'll let you contact the President personally and that's when you'll offer him the package."

"How's offering up Yasmina and Serosa going to help the situation?" asked Attorney Standridge.

"You see, once he knows that he's exposed and someone with some clout is onto him, he'll agree to meet on your terms and that's when you'll record everything he says."

The plan seemed like a solid one, but something plagued the attorney.

"If I agree to do this, meet with the President, after I've told him that I have proof that he's up to no good, don't you think he will try to have me killed? I mean, my gosh, the man will have Secret Service agents for miles around him."

Again, Dalvin laughed. "That's the point. I know he'll try and have you killed but leave that end to me and I'll have you covered." Looking to both Damita and Attorney Standridge he said, "I'm gon'go stash these two dudes somewhere safe until we get in touch with the President and set a date. We'll use a photo of both men as evidence to back up our claims and once the deal is done and we have the President where we want him, I'll get rid of these bodies, we'll get Yasmina and Serosa back safely and we'll have the President facing a jury."

When the attorney agreed, Dalvin thought, *I'll kill that muthafucka the first chance I get.* But the words that came out were, "Once we start the ball rolling, there's ***NO WAY OUT***!"

CHAPTER TWENTY-THREE

CLICHY, FRANCE

They stood huddled under an awning at a restaurant - Le Rebuchon. The weather was warm this time of year but the rain blowing in from the River La Seine brought in a chill.

"This place is beautiful," Yasmina said as they were led to a table in a corner.

It was the first day she'd taken a full tour of the city. Without fear of being spotted due in part to her new hair cut, she exuded confidence in a Prada dress with a black shawl draped over her shoulders and a pair of matching pumps.

Yasmina clung to Giddeon as they visited various landmarks in the quaint city.

"You're the one who's beautiful!" Giddeon countered, causing Yasmina to blush. She couldn't stop thinking about the night she'd had with him. Grabbing a menu, she buried her face into it.

"I think I'll leave the ordering to you." Just then a waiter arrived.

The girl looked young to Yasmina, she couldn't have been any older than twenty. As she stared at her, thoughts of Serosa came to mind. The thoughts vanished when she overheard Giddeon say, "Si, Coquilles Saint Jacques, sur un lit de meschun." The waiter scribbled orders on a pad. Feeling a bit out of touch with the language, Yasmina perused the menu but couldn't find the dish Giddeon selected. He continued.

"For the Madame, loup braised et risotto de truffles, y Pouilly Fuisse 1966."

Finally and only when she was sure Giddeon had completed the order, Yasmina cleared her throat.

"Uh-hum!"

Giddeon eyed her. "What?" he smiled.

"What in the hell was that? I hope you didn't order me fish eggs and snail 'cause all that mumbo jumbo you were speaking, I know it had to have one of those in it." They both shared a hearty laugh.

"Well, for starters," Giddeon pointed at an item on the menu, "I ordered both of us grilled scallops on a fresh meschun salad."

"Meschun," Yasmina wrinkled her nose. "What's that?"

"Meschun salad is young, tender, greens. In America I think you guys call it. . ." he searched for the equivalent, "…cabbage, or turnip greens." Pointing to another item, Giddeon added, "For the main course I ordered sea bass with risotto and a bottle of White Burgundy Wine 1966."

Impressed, Yasmina smiled. "Do you treat all your women like this?"

The words came so fast Yasmina couldn't stop them. She placed a hand over her mouth, but the damage was done.

"I'm so sorry, Giddeon," she managed to say out of embarrassment. "I didn't mean for it to sound the way it did." In fact Yasmina was beginning to grow fond of Giddeon. She hadn't spent much time, or any time, with a man so charming and compassionate in the last ten years.

"No problem," Giddeon assured Yasmina as he placed his hand on hers.

He too was beginning to develop feelings. It'd been years since he felt this way and with their wonderful night last night, he thought about approaching Yasmina about her future.

"Since we're on the subject of personal lives," he eyed her, "there is something I want to ask you."

Giddeon was somewhat shocked when Yasmina changed the subject.

"I wonder when I will get the chance to see my daughter."

The comment startled Giddeon. "You never mentioned the reason this guy, Shotty Dread, was after you." Yasmina didn't respond.

CHAPTER TWENTY-FOUR

Yasmina and Giddeon walked the streets in silence. Darkness had swallowed what was left of the day and the only light came from streetlights, or an occasional reflection from a vehicle as it sped past. As they neared the entrance to the underground subway, Giddeon clutched Yasmina's hand. For seconds both lingered, staring into each other's eyes, no words being spoken. Then Giddeon leaned forward, his mouth covering Yasmina's, and they shared a long, passionate kiss.

The sound of a train racing up the tube, its metal wheels grinding, broke the romantic moment. Giddeon wasted no time as he turned to face Yasmina.

"So are you going to answer my question?"

Yasmina faced the window. She had a hard time trusting people. The only person she loved enough to give her entire heart to abandoned her when he died. Now that she'd found someone for the time being to filled voids in her life that had been present for the last decade, she wasn't sure if she was ready to open her heart up, much less talk about her past.

When Giddeon tilted Yasmina's face back in his direction, he was shocked to find her in tears.

"Hey," he said in a soothing tone. "If you don't want to talk about it, it's fine. I'm sorry, I didn't mean to seem forceful."

Yasmina smiled through her tears.

"It's not you. It's just, this is really the first time in ten years that I have spoken freely about the relationship I had with Scorcher. In prison, I was busy trying to defend myself against attacks from staff members."

The train had stopped, departed, stopped, and departed numerous times. Yasmina spoke freely, telling Giddeon everything from when she first met Damita, her attraction that led to marriage with Scorcher, and how Shotty Dread chased them from Jamaica to Florida. When she was finished, Giddeon could only nod his head.

"So you see," Yasmina continued, "I think Shotty Dread still has a vendetta and now that he has Serosa, he'll use her as bait to get me."

Giddeon knew Yasmina was in a fragile state. He didn't want to heap too much on her so he changed the subject.

"These other men, the ones who chased you into the building, and the man who called your phone, why do you think they're after you?"

Yasmina didn't have an answer. Even though she knew, she didn't tell him. Then the memory of the Senator's visit with her while she waited on death row, came to mind.

"For some odd reason, I think it has everything to do with that man," Yasmina whispered. "And if we could find out who he is, I think he'll reveal everything we need to know."

Exiting through the doors of the train, Giddeon stopped Yasmina. He grabbed both her hands.

"Look, I know you barely know anything about me, but I'm not going to hide the fact that I care about you."

Yasmina gently placed her index finger to his lips stopping him in mid-sentence.

"I know, let's get my daughter back first."

The train departed, screeching its wheels as it sped off.

CHAPTER TWENTY-FIVE

THE NEXT DAY

The Mini Cooper had just driven onto the A-1 Autoroute when Giddeon's phone vibrated.

"Speak!" he said, not taking his eyes off traffic as he flew down the road.

After the person on the other end gave the code, "PLATINUM CHICK," he passed the phone to Yasmina.

"Hello," she said, even though she had no clue who waited on the other end.

For seconds there was silence. The hum of the car passing other vehicles was the only sound until she heard,

"Whatever you do just act normal." Yasmina wrinkled her face.

"Damita, what's wrong?"

Damita continuously glanced over her shoulders. Though she sat facing the window and the door, she couldn't stop thinking that someone was following her. She was in a coffee shop. Not wasting any time, she went into detail about the two men who'd barged into her home and held her at gunpoint. "I think I know the reason they're after you and Serosa." After explaining what she'd learned form the men she added, "And the guys claim to work for the Vice President of the United States, who in turn works for. . ."

"Let me guess," Yasmina interrupted, "the President."

Yasmina couldn't believe this. As the thought of being caught in some government corruption she had nothing to do with entered her mind, she clenched her teeth. She was angry at first but felt better after she learned what she was up against.

"It's all coming together!" she screamed, startling both Giddeon, and Damita.

The call from Damita and the information she'd given came at a time when Yasmina was beginning to have serious doubts. Many nights she contemplated going to the authorities and turning herself in but the fact still remained Serosa would still be in danger of Shotty Dread and the President. After talking a few minutes more with Damita, Yasmina learned something else.

"Yes, I still hadn't heard anything from Serosa since Shotty Dread took her to Europe and to be honest, I don't think he wants to harm her. Why would he leave us alive?"

Yasmina's silence caused Giddeon to stare in her direction.

"Is everything alright?"

Even though she gave no answer, Yasmina shot Giddeon a look. She'd just finished speaking with Damita.

"I don't know," she said, "but I can honestly say from what I've just learned, we're involved in some deep shit and it's scary to think about who's involved."

Yasmina ran down the information she'd received from Damita. She then expanded on the fact that Damita hadn't heard from Shotty Dread or Serosa since leaving the country.

Giddeon shrugged his shoulders.

"What's next? I mean, what're we going to do now that we know some or most of the players involved in this game?"

Yasmina flashed a piece of paper; a smirk came to her face.

"What's that?"

"It's Shotty Dread's number," she said plainly.

"When are you going to call?"

"Now's a better time than ever since his ass didn't get back to me like he said he would."

The phone was nearing its third ring when she looked at Giddeon.

"Right about now, Damita's cousin, Dalvin, is dialing the number to the President of the United States," she said. Giddeon was in shock.

CHAPTER TWENTY-SIX

WASHINGTON, D.C.

Tinkerton was seated in the Oval Office in a heated discussion with the President. He'd been there since seven that morning and the two still had not reached an agreement that would appease both of them; he was ready to throw in the towel.

Unfolding his legs Tinkerton stood up when he felt something twitter inside the pocket of his jacket. He took a brief glance at his phone realizing he didn't know the number. Disregarding the call, Tinkerton put the phone on a table next to his chair.

President L'Enfants was getting annoyed.

"For Christ's sake, are you going to take the call or what?"

The phone was now vibrating across the smooth surface of the table. Tinkerton finally answered. The President eavesdropped but couldn't follow the conversation. The President knew it was bad news as he watched Tinkerton loosen his tie as if he couldn't get enough air. When the conversation was over Tinkerton said, "That was my wife; problems at home, you know."

As much he wished it was really his wife calling, Tinkerton couldn't remove the words of the caller: "Look here, muthafucka, either you call the number that I'm sure is visible on your screen in five minutes, or you don't. It doesn't matter to me one way or another. You're the one who'll be going down and if you're smart, you might not want to take this ride by yourself."

The loud smack of President L'Enfants's hand against the table snapped Tinkerton out of his thoughts.

"Damn it!" he yelled. "Your wife must've told you she was packing up and leaving you. You're sweating like a bunch of honeybees have gotten a hold of your ass!"

With a sheepish expression on his face, Tinkerton mumbled, "I wish it was that simple."

XXXXXXXXXXX

"Who is this?" Tinkerton asked, suspicious of the man answering on the first ring.

He was now on a secured line, electing to tell the President that he needed to go home and handle the situation with his wife.

Traffic on 16th street was busy. Cars, trucks, and pedestrians went about their day. In Tinkerton's eyes, every person walking by, looking over the rim of their glasses, or driving by at a slow speed, was guilty. He knew how the government worked.

And for this exact reason, Tinkerton nervously glanced around as he stood in front of the phone booth.

"Introductions aren't necessary," the man aggressively spat. "Just know I know who you are and what you're into, and there are other important people - judges, lawyers, prosecutors - who will soon learn the things I know about you, and your boss, the President, if you are not willing to make a wise decision."

Tinkerton was beside himself. "How did you get this number?"

"I'll put it like this," Dalvin said. "A lot of skin had to melt and peel, not to mention a lot of pain was endured, before I learned of your deceit. Is this how all the politicians running for office work, I mean, involved in murder, extortion, coercion, scandals?"

The words stung but Tinkerton knew the accusations were true. He now regretted ever bribing the President for the job.

"What is it that you want from me?"

Dalvin sucked his teeth. He could hear fear in the man's voice.

"Now, what makes you think I want something from you?" he teased.

Dalvin was enjoying this moment. There weren't many chances when he was able to stick it to government officials; the DEA being the group he really wished was at the end of the rope, but he'd settle for the catch he had.

Tinkerton was growing more impatient by the second.

"Look, you're the one who contacted me. Now if games are what you called to play, I'll gladly hang up and you'll never hear from me again."

"You won't do shit!" Dalvin laughed, daring the man. He knew the moment Tinkerton called back, he had him. "What you gon' do is listen to what I have to say and when I'm finished, you're going to agree with everything I say." He paused for a second, "Do I make myself clear?"

"Yeah," Tinkerton mumbled.

"I didn't hear that, what?"

"Yes. Damn!"

"Good!" Dalvin smiled. "If I thought you said otherwise, I wouldn't hesitate to turn what I have in to the people I mentioned earlier. And I don't think that pretty little wife of yours would be too happy when she sees your face on television being charged with everything I've already named, and kidnapping."

When the word "kidnapping" left Dalvin's mouth, the line went silent.

Tinkerton had to think. With his hand pressed against his forehead, he ran his fingers through his hair. "Now wait!" Tinkerton managed to stammer, shifting from foot to foot. "Kidnapping. . . I . . . I didn't participate in any kidnapping."

Dalvin's laugh caused Tinkerton to ask, "What's so funny?"

"Sounds like I have your attention now, huh?" Dalvin laughed. He didn't bother to respond to Tinkerton's comment. Instead he added, "If you have knowledge of who's holding the girl and the woman it would be in your best interest to see to it that they make it home safely by tomorrow at noon." Tinkerton was about to speak when

Dalvin cut him off. "I'm not finished yet. I already know you're responsible for the murder of my best friend and his family; the men who work for you told me that much." Dalvin could hear Tinkerton swallow the lump in his throat. He continued. "We can't cry over what's already done but you, my friend, you can possibly exonerate yourself by helping me bring down your boss."

"That's impossible. . . "

"Is it?" asked Dalvin.

"Well, I mean, it's not impossible," Tinkerton reconsidered, "but it won't be easy. I mean, if I decided to take you up on your offer."

Dalvin suddenly became serious.

"Look here, muthafucka, this contract ain't about if; the deal is going down now. If I hang this phone up and you haven't agreed to my terms, expect to have a visit from your own people, and it won't be about the mortgage crisis or the recession this country is going through, catch my drift?"

When Tinkerton agreed, Dalvin ran down a list of demands.

CHAPTER TWENTY-SEVEN

Weeks had passed. Henry hadn't heard a single word from the police about the abduction of his family. He was tired of trying to get information from the authorities. He'd lost all faith in the justice system and was beginning to accept the possibility that his family was dead.

The last conversation he'd had with anyone connected to the case was weeks ago. The phone rang; Henry hoped it was Detective Genarski phoning him with some news about his family.

"Hello!" he answered anxiously, pressing the receiver against his ear.

When he didn't hear a response his hopes faded knowing if it were the detective, he would have spoken by then. Just as

Henry was about to curse the unidentified caller out, then a familiar voice spoke.

Immediately, he realized it was the same man who abducted his wife and daughter. He clenched the phone. "You son of a bitch!" Henry belted. "Where is my family?"

Gaietho laughed, truth be told he was nervous. For the last few weeks, he'd been in and out of hotels, sleeping in abandoned houses and shelters. At one point, he was sure he was being followed after he noticed two men in a sedan, like the one that ran interference when Cary and Brittany were kidnapped. Fearing he didn't have long before his former employer's mercenaries attempted to take him out, he made a desperate move - one he knew would either have him arrested on the spot or killed. As he listened to the frustration and anger in Henry's voice, he understood that arrogance and cockiness wasn't the way to achieve what he hoped for in making the call. So instead, with all the humility he could muster, he said, "Henry, I know right now you must hate my guts..."

Henry didn't give him a chance to complete his sentence before saying, "Hate your guts?! You son of a bitch, if I get my hands on you, I'm gonna show you how much I hate you."

After letting Henry vent, Gaietho managed to offer, "I can't dispute your hatred for me and what I did to your family, Henry. But if you want to get them back, I think we have to work together and put our differences aside for the moment."

Henry wrinkled his face. He couldn't fathom working with the same man who abducted his family, and murdered his best friend.

"Are you saying what I think you are?" he said.

"Yes," Gaietho said. "Now is time for us to become friends of circumstance."

Henry remained quiet, hesitating before saying, "What makes you think I need your help in getting my family back?"

Thinking about the question, Gaietho uttered, "Well, if you don't need my assistance, I'll just end this call and you never have to hear from me again."

"Hold up!" Henry interrupted. "All I'm saying is, how do I know you're not just saying this to get close to me so you can murder another person who can identify you?"

"Henry," Gaietho said confidently, "if I wanted to do that, you would've been shot dead yesterday morning as you retrieved the morning paper from just outside your door."

Henry swallowed a huge lump that burned his throat. Now on his feet, he ran to the window-brushing the curtains aside. After frantically looking in each direction, his heart raced as he watched the mailman pull away from his mailbox.

"You, you were watching me?"

"I know, Henry," Gaietho laughed, "you can't believe that I watched you do your morning ritual. It's part of my job, Henry, that's how I make a living."

After running down to Henry that his intentions were not to hurt him, he ended the call but not before saying, "Working together, we can bring the President down. I'll be a witness, and testify about everything I was ordered to do for him but I'll need you to do your part."

As the dial tone buzzed in his ears, Henry still couldn't believe he'd just spoken with the man who murdered his friend and abducted his family. *I made a deal with an assassin, the devil, he thought to himself.*

Deep in thought, Henry was distracted as he noticed a woman on the television, a news reporter, standing on the Anacostia River Bridge reporting something as divers and police scoured the murky waters below. He turned the volume up.

"Police still have no clues as to the whereabouts of a mother and daughter, missing for the last few weeks. It is believed that Cary and Brittany Landsford were kidnapped for money but authorities can't seem to find any leads or clues that point to any specific person of interest in this case. The father and husband of the females, Henry Landsford, was employed by St. Bonaventures Girls Reform School and it is believed that he was possibly targeted by unknown assailants."

He sat in disappointment and disbelief that they hadn't heard anything by now. "Why are they saying this is about money?" he yelled. He knew that Gaietho didn't kidnap them for money. "Damn it! I specifically told that detective my family was kidnapped by a man with a thick Middle Eastern accent. They then were taken by some agents, who I found out were working for the Vice President. Why would he lie to the media and say the abduction was about money?"

Henry was almost in tears. He was about to change the channel when the reporter said, "Divers are combing the Anacostia River." There was a knock at the door. Henry's first thought was reporters. They'd been camping in front of his house since the investigation began and he'd had enough of answering the same questions. Irritated, he got up and headed for the door when the reporter added, “This just in, it is believed that divers have found--”

Knock! Knock! Knock!

The raps at the door were getting louder. Henry debated whether to answer the door or continue listening to the reporter.

“For the life of me!” he shouted.

Slowly, Henry backed toward the door, his steps dragging as his eyes remained glued to the television.

“Wait, they have found something.”

Henry was almost there. His sweaty palms clutched the doorknob but his eyes stayed glued to the tube.

Without even bothering to glance over his shoulder, Henry twisted the knob.

“For Christ’s sake, can you people please! “

Just as the words left his mouth, the reporter screamed,“Divers have found a body, no, two bodies. . .”

Henry’s world was crushed. He knew his family had been found in the bottom of the river. As tears of sorrow gushed from his eyes, he wasn’t aware of the arms wrapping around his body until he heard two voices cry out to him.

Brittany, Cary,” he stammered in disbelief, seeing his family standing before him, “my gosh, you’re alive!”

CHAPTER TWENTY-EIGHT

"We need to talk," President L'Enfants said to Tinkerton. He remained hesitant as he stood in the door way. "Come in, close the door and take a seat."

The President nodded his head in the direction of an antique chair sitting in the middle of the room. He watched as his Vice President leisurely walked past the chair, stopped in front of a sound system mounted against the wall, turned some music on and sat in the chair.

"You're implying that you don't trust me?" the President chuckled. He raised an eyebrow. "That's really rude, don't play that while we talk."

"I'm only assuring that this conversation remains between us," Tinkerton replied, "What is it?"

President L'Enfants leaned back in his seat. He couldn't believe the audacity of the man sitting in front of him.

"I'll get straight down to business. I'd like to know what you are doing and where you are on the situation with Gaietho."

Tinkerton crossed his legs and exhaled. "Well, sir, he hasn't surfaced anywhere. It is believed that he fled the country or has assumed one of his various other identities."

"Uh-huh!" President L'Enfants grumbled. "What about the woman and the child?"

Hearing this caused Tinkerton's throat to get dry. He'd watched the news earlier on and knew that two bodies had been found in the Anacostia River. He also knew that by now the President had gotten wind of the situation and was merely feeling him out. Tinkerton swallowed hard. "Give me a few more hours, after I speak with my men, and I'll have an answer for you."

This was nothing more than a stall tactic. Tinkerton knew if he could convince the President that everything was going according to planned, and nothing could come back to haunt him, the President would give him what he needed. With his back in a corner and Dalvin breathing down his neck, he wanted to make sure he got all the incriminating evidence he could on President L'Enfants. Having worked for the President for the last eight years, Tinkerton knew how he operated. He also realized that he was trying to distance himself to protect his own ass, even if it meant hanging Tinkerton out to dry.

"The last matter I wanted to ask you about was the young girl, Serosa. . ." his pause was enough to make sure he had Tinkerton's undivided attention. "Tell me that you've taken care of the situation."

Tinkerton read between the lines; he clearly knew the meaning and the consequences of such a remark. Shifting uneasily in his seat, he felt inside his jacket and pulled out a white handkerchief.

"Look, Mr. President," Tinkerton yelled, "you're not making this any easier. I mean, I have people on my end scrambling, combing every inch of the country for these people. My contacts have gone from North Carolina to Portland. . ." he suddenly paused as memories of what Dalvin had done to his men in Portland surfaced. He continued shortly afterwards, "...trying to tie up loose ends, something you should've taken care of when you first decided to get yourself involved in murder and God knows what else."

Tinkerton was furious. He'd let his emotions get out of control. He stood to his feet.

"Goodness, can't you just call the hitman you've hired and square things away? I'm quite sure in order to get his life back he'd be willing to take care of the situation just as he did when you hired him to murder. Dr. Carmichael." The entire time Tinkerton spoke, the President moved closer to him. By the time Tinkerton had realized anything, President L'Enfants was frisking him.

"Edgar," Tinkerton belted in disbelief, "you, you think I'm wearing a wire or something? Do you think I'm trying to set you up?"

Speaking mildly the President confessed, "It's me, Adam, I hired an assassin. I had the girl and her mother kidnapped. Hell, I even had Dr. Carmichael murdered."

Tinkerton stared into his eyes he saw something sinister. The President continued. "It wouldn't surprise me if you were wearing a wire, son. Look at our history; you bribed me into giving you your position. I wouldn't be surprised if you were a whistle-blower, working with people who don't give a damn about you."

When the President paused, Tinkerton started thinking. *Does he know about my association with Dalvin?* Before anymore thoughts could fester, the President added,

"Take our history, or the history of America, do you think power and riches came from honest work? No, it didn't. It came from the blood, sweat, and tears of others. Hell, they had to walk through fire brimstone but they succeeded. You tuck your tail and run as fast as you can at the first sign of trouble."

The words stung. Each syllable expressed was like a needle being stuck in Tinkerton's body but the President didn't hold back.

"I admit I've done a lot of things that weren't by the book. I've stolen money, locked away people I knew were innocent and even murdered to protect my family," the President confessed. "Adam, you don't get it. There's a bigger picture than what you see."

Tinkerton only stared, he couldn't speak. He couldn't believe what he was hearing, although he was glad to have the confession on tape.

President L'Enfants continued. "That's why we were never good together. We're cut from different cloths. Me, I'm what you call genuine leather. I endure through the toughest of times, there's not many like me left."

As Tinkerton stared at the man, he shook his head in disbelief. Having heard enough, Tinkerton started to leave when the President grabbed his arm. His heart started pumping. Tinkerton knew he needed to get out of the building and get the tape into the necessary hands. "Do you remember her? The President asked, handing a piece of paper to Tinkerton.

"I don't recall."

"Well, two years before I became a senator in Florida, this young lady was facing a death sentence for murder and distribution of drugs. She's been locked up for ten years." He waited to see if Tinkerton recollected anything. He added, "Well, she was my first pardon as President."

The expression on Tinkerton's face was indescribable. "You , you!" he stammered. "She was part of the crew Yasmina created, The Platinum Chicks. You freed her so she could kill. .."

"Adam, immunity is power and in the right hands you can do things God only imagined." The door clicked shut.

CHAPTER TWENTY-NINE

The meeting was set for eight o'clock. Tinkerton had managed to carry out one of three things Dalvin had instructed him to do and the second act depended upon his arrival.

Henry couldn't keep his eyes off of Dalvin. They were huddled in the living room; Henry, his wife, Cary, and Dalvin, listening as Dalvin explained going to the police wasn't an option.

"Listen, lady," Dalvin stated with finality. He'd had it up to his neck trying to convince the tormented woman that he was one of the good guys. "I'm not the one you should be worried about. From the information I've already gathered, this shit involves public figures. Hell, I had to damn near melt one of the guy's eyes out in order to make his partner tell me what they knew."

Not bothering to conceal the gory details of torture, Dalvin spoke freely with no regard to the effect it was having on Cary but Henry noticed it.

"Listen, Cary," he grabbed both of her shoulders. "I know this seems farfetched but I think he's right." Henry's eyes found Dalvin. "Besides, he's the reason you're back home safely."

Confident that things were under control, Dalvin continued. "Now, we already know that this President has a lot of contacts in the Secret Service and possibly every police precinct in Northern Virginia and all of Maryland. And if I'm correct, we're further placing ourselves in danger of being exposed, if not killed, if we go running to them with what we know."

"Well, what do you propose?" Cary asked. "Sit here and wait and we're making ourselves targets, and Brittany's had enough already!" she yelled.

Henry was about to interject when Dalvin raised a hand. He moved to Cary's side.

"Look, Mrs. . .?"

"Lansford," Cary sobbed.

"Mrs. Lansford," Dalvin repeated. "I know what you're going through; these people murdered my friend and his family. They even came to my home but fortunately I'd already gotten wind of the situation." Carey dried her eyes. "Now, there's a guy I'm depending on to deliver what we will need as evidence that could be used against the President."

"Here!" Cary interrupted, "Isn't it already dangerous enough?"

"Believe me," Dalvin tried to soothe Cary, his hand patting gently against her arm. "I understand your concerns but yes, this is the right place."

After explaining how fortunate they were that there were cameras crews around when they arrived, he added, "There's no way someone would try anything while those people are camping outside. "

Carey was convinced only after she moved to the window and found three news vans parked in front of her door. There was something still bothering her.

"This person, the man you say you're waiting for, who is he? Why do you think you can trust him?" A smirk came to Dalvin's face.

"Well, Mrs. Lansford, this man doesn't want to spend the rest of his young life in prison. More importantly, he's the Vice President of the United States."

Both Cary's and Henry's mouths fell open.

CHAPTER THIRTY

It was the commotion outside that caused Dalvin, Henry and his wife, Cary, to bolt for the window. They'd been engulfed in formulating strategies that it didn't dawn on them that eight o'clock had come and gone minutes ago. As they stared through the darkness of night, they weren't able to clearly see what the clamor was about until Dalvin saw the news van door open and a lady reporter rush to get out. The man sat inside his car, a silver Chrysler 300m, something that fit his modest style of living. To the untrained eye, it appeared to be any old vehicle, but the lady reporter knew differently. She'd seen this car once before and knew it to be the car of the Vice President of the United States. The diplomat tag in the front was a dead give away.

Nervously, Dalvin watched as the reporter and a few members from one of the other news vans, walked closer. The car's door was cracked, causing a dim light to flash. Dalvin watched as the Vice President bent over coughing.

"Mr. Vice President, are you alright?" the reporter asked. She stood a few inches away, a worried look on her face. The raspy and dry coughs continued. Tinkerton, although he'd heard the voice, was unable to speak, his face buried in a white handkerchief. With all the vigor he could muster, he struggled from the car. The coughing hadn't subsided, it seemed to get worse. Neighbors and onlookers walked up to Henry's front yard to see what was going on.

Seeing this, Dalvin shook his head. He thought he had every angle covered. When he told the Vice President to meet at Henry's, he felt safer. The neighborhood was located in a prominent section of town; doctors, professors, judges and attorneys lived there. It was almost a guaranteed location. As he pushed his way through the crowd of frantic people, some running around crying, others panicking looking for emergency aids to come fly down the street, he realized this was the last place to invite someone of Tinkerton's status.

Tinkerton was on his back, wheezing. Though it was dark, his purple face stood out in the dim neighborhood lights like a plump grape. It was then that it dawned on Dalvin that someone had gotten to him. While the crowd gathered, no doctor coming to the rescue, Dalvin kneeled over Tinkerton's body. His lips moved slowly as he struggled to tell Dalvin something. "In my left breast pocket is the.... "He never finished his sentence. His words trailed off as his final breath escaped his lungs. He was pronounced dead at 8:15p.m.

Dalvin couldn't believe what happened. Though he had incriminating evidence that could be used against the President, he knew he still faced an uphill battle. He grabbed his cell phone.

"Yeah, it's me," he said after hearing Damita's voice. "Look," he continued, "I can't talk long. It's a lot of shit going on and the only way to handle these problems is to bring it to our turf."

Damita wrinkled her face. "What do you mean-bring it to our turf?"

"Just watch the news in the next half hour and you'll know exactly what I mean, until then, do everything in your power to get in touch with Yasmina. They're in danger, real danger and you need to warn them."

CHAPTER THIRTY-ONE

MARSEILLES, FRANCE

"Mi see ya finally gathered the nerves to ring me, Yasmina."

Shotty Dread was seated outside of his chateau's carriage house watching a herd of Arabian stallions gallop the length of the expansive hillside, a three hundred acre ranch he'd purchased years before his incarceration.

"Yasmina," he teased, "wha' took ya so long? Mi though you would wanta set'tle dis matter quickly."

"Well," Yasmina began, finally finding her voice, "my reason for delay isn't what's important. You're holding on to something that belongs to me and I want her back."

Making it to this point was a tremendous feat in itself. For as long as Yasmina could remember, or at least the last ten years, she wanted to face the man and tell him how much she hated him. The memory of the meeting she'd had with him - being chased across the country, having to bury people she loved because of him - left hate in her heart. Now there was a purpose worth dying for. If facing her fears head on was what it was going to take to get Serosa back, she was more than willing to confront the source of her angst. Shotty Dread would've liked nothing more to engage Yasmina in a battle over the phone but there were more pressing issues to deal with.

"In downtown Paris, there is a monument called Arc de Triomphe. It's located at the south end of Champs-Elysees. Meet me there at six o'clock today."

Before Yasmina could get a question in, the dial tone buzzed in her ears.

XXXXXXX

The Mini-Cooper sped along with traffic as it exited onto an off ramp. After crossing the River La Seine, Giddeon merged onto Champs-Elysees Avenue.

Looking around, Yasmina sighed. *This will be like finding a needle in a hay stack,* she thought, shocked by the hundreds of tourists.

Once out of the vehicle, they made their way over to the Arc de Triomphe. "Do you remember what he looks like?" asked Giddeon. Yasmina didn't bother responding. She was too consumed with searching the crowd hoping somehow to catch a glimpse of the man she hadn't seen in over ten years. Sadly she saw no one resembling Shotty Dread, at least as she remembered him.

"What's wrong?" Giddeon asked, finding Yasmina frozen. "Did you see him?"

For moments Yasmina stared ahead, here eyes fixed on someone standing not to far away. It was only when a large-red tour bus blocked her view did Yasmina snap out of her trance. The woman was gone.

Again, Giddeon asked, "Yasmina, are you okay enough to go through with this?" his hand gently resting against her arm. "If you aren't, you can call--"

"No!" Yasmina interrupted. "I'm ok. I thought I saw someone I knew from my past but it can't be." She shrugged the thought off. "Anyways, the last time I saw Shotty Dread, he walked with a limp and a cane. He's short, maybe an inch or two shorter than me and his dreads hang past his waistline. That was over ten years ago, who knows what he looks like today."

They waited at the entrance of the Arc de Triomphe. Yasmina was nervous. She shifted from one foot to the other and glanced from face to face as her eyes scanned the crowd of people.

The once massive crowd of anxious tourists was thinning, people slowly trickling inside to view the structure. Yasmina wore a grey outfit she'd picked up while shopping - a black-waist length leather coat draped over her shoulders concealing the handbag latched to her arm.

He saw her, he was sure of it, even though her hair was styled differently. *Maybe she had it cut to change her appearance,* the man thought as he watched the young lady head back toward his vehicle. When she opened the door-stepping back inside the car, he said, "What do you think?"

"I can't be sure," the woman replied, "but if we were to use my guess, I'd say it's her."

The man smiled casually as he had when receiving the report that his sniper had succeeded in flushing Yasmina out of the room. He grabbed his phone and dialed a number.

"I'm already here!" was all the voice said. She hadn't thought about anyone else calling.

"Your five days are up!" the voice said. Looking to the woman seated beside him, he passed her a .9mm with a silencer.

"It's her!"

CHAPTER THIRTY-TWO

Neither Yasmina nor Giddeon knew what to make of the situation. They both knew it was the same man who called while Yasmina was being held up in the safe house back in Switzerland. "How did he get this number?" Giddeon asked, puzzled.

"How'd he know we were in Paris?" Yasmina countered with another question.

Coming up with no rational answer that would either of them, Yasmina said, "Whoever this person is, we'll deal with him later." She pointed to her watch it was 6:17 p.m. "I gotta see what's taking Shotty Dread so long."

After dialing Shotty Dread's number, Yasmina realized he was on the third floor waiting on her. She fumbled with her bag. "It's now or never," she eyed Giddeon, "but one way or another, I'll get my daughter back."

The elevator stopped on the third floor. Tourists were packed on the elevator like sardines, waiting for their floor. Through all of the talking, Yasmina spotted an unmistakable raspy voice that had haunted her for years.

"Yasmina, prison has done you good these last ten years!"

At first the sound startled Yasmina. Too many people were milling around, she couldn't put a face to the voice. As the crowd parted, she saw him. Yasmina's first inclination was to shoot the bastard but she thought better of it. She still hadn't seen Serosa; she wondered if she would even recognize her.

While Yasmina was deep in thought, something got her attention. The woman she'd seen earlier was back, watching her. As the crowd continued to thin out, Yasmina heard Shotty Dread say, "What ya say we work out're differences so everyone is happy?" He glared at Yasmina as he moved his motorized wheelchair closer.

Yasmina suddenly felt dizzy. The voices around her were muffled, she couldn't understand a word anyone was saying. The only Yasmina knew was that Serosa was in danger. She was also in danger and the only way to protect herself was to remove Shotty Dread - permanently. Yasmina thought she was face to face with the devil.

Everything was a blur. Yasmina couldn't remember when she pulled her gun out or when the once crowded room seemed to clear out. The only thing real to her was shoving the barrel of her.25 automatic into Shotty Dread's face; if she killed the head of the snake, the body would soon follow.

Shotty Dread was surprised by Yasmina's actions. "What ya gwan do dat for, woman? Now, look'a what ya done?"

The cold tone of his voice brought Yasmina back to reality. She could now hear the whimpers and cries of tourists who were huddled against the walls, some frantically punched keys of the elevator in hopes that it would open up and lead them to safety.

Giddeon was shocked by how cold-hearted Shotty Dread was. People were running for cover, begging for their lives, and crying out of fear, but Shotty Dread didn't seem to give a shit. His face was blank. This quick assessment revealed to Giddeon many things about the man. Shotty Dread was used to conflict, adverse situations and danger. It was something Giddeon realized could be deadly for Yasmina if she underestimated Shotty Dread's capabilities.

As if Shotty Dread somehow read Giddeon's mind, he looked at them and brushed the gun Yasmina held to his head away like it was a gnat.

"The way I see tings, Yasmina, you 'ave less than twenty minutes before Sheriff John Brown and his deputies come busting thru dat door." He pointed at the stairwell entrance. "Now, I 'ave a couple of men posted downstairs making sure no one comes thru de elevator door, so," his eyes scanned Yasmina's, who had raised the gun back to his head. "What 'tis it goon' be?
You 'ave two choices to make," Shotty Dread continued. "One, you can pull that trigger and not listen to what I 'ave to tell ya, and two," his eyes searched hers for emotion. "You can listen to me speak about something important to both you and Serosa, then decide if you still want to kill me before the bumble clot lawman comes to arrest both of us. It's your choice to make!"

EPILOGUE

The weeks following the funeral put a tremendous load of stress on Serosa. Now, as she watched tubes and machines prolong her mother's life, she couldn't help feeling like she was facing a curse of death somewhere down the short bloodline of her family. Yasmina's signs of making it were bleak. The ventilator hissed each time it breathed life into her body. Her chest inflated then deflated. She looked as if she was in a peaceful sleep.

The diagnosis the surgeon left with Serosa, Giddeon and Brandon, wasn't good. "We'll be lucky if she survives through the night." A look of sorrow crossed his face. He then added, "After 13 hours of surgery, we were able to mend her spine but more than likely she will never be able to walk again. The bullet severed a spinal nerve, and she lost a lot of blood." The surgeon paused a moment to let the words sink in. Removing his sweaty head cover, he brushed his hair to the side. "Now that she's stabilized and the bleeding has subsided, the only thing we can do is wait." Nodding, he turned and walked away.

That was three weeks ago. Now, Serosa attentively sat beside her mother's hospital bed and soaked up every word her raspy voice could utter. She was thankful that God had given her mother another chance at life, even though Yasmina was paralyzed from the waist down. Their happy moments were interrupted when three people barged in.

"The doctor says my mom can't have any visitors outside of the family," Serosa snapped, moving to stand n front of the men. When she realized who one of the men was, she smirked, her hand covering her mouth. The man was an attorney - Jan Juneau. Serosa had become familiar with him while in the presence of Shotty Dread. Jan Juneau represented clients, famous and not, who owned huge estates. He also drafted wills and other important documents that pertained to wealth.

Yasmina watched as the man rifle through a black leather briefcase. She could hear the rough paper scratching. After he found what he was looking for the attorney gestured toward the other two men who came with him. "These gentlemen aren't with me, they're with the police Nationale." The guys immediately flashed badges.

Not only did Yasmina's pulse quicken, but Serosa and Brandon also got nervous. They were familiar with the French police force. The name was repeated more than once when they thought they were trapped inside of the hotel room.

The attorney started reading from a stack of papers. "It is here that I, Osei Love Sr., father of Anthony Osei "Scorcher" Love Jr., and grandfather of Serosa Love...." Both Yasmina's and Serosa's eyes met. They were shocked. Yasmina started to speak only to be silenced by the attorney. "Please, let me finish and then everything will become clear to everyone.

"...bequeath all my valuables; money, real estate properties, businesses to the parties mentioned throughout this will, when I am deceased. In dispensing my will, I would also like to grant Serosa, sole heir, my estate here in France, $270 Million dollar and the power to do as she pleases with corporations I own. She is the only living blood relative in the Love family and all of my possessions will be awarded to her."

The attorney continued reading despite the murmurs going around the room.

"It is also at this time that I, Osei Love Sr., would like to offer my sincerest apologies to the one person I never had the chance to know. Yasmina, I am truly sorry for the tremendous pain I've caused you, and your family and friends. I've managed to cause you great suffering and loss by some of the things I've done in my life.

In the lifestyle that I have lived since age thirteen we were taught that when people feared you, it was power. Throughout my life I've manifested that power and turned a nickel and dime hustle into a thriving billion dollar empire. I'm not saying this to gloat, or to be an excuse for the things I've done in my life time, but I'm merely stating that, it was all I knew. And certainly after losing almost everyone in my family, with the exception of finding that I had a granddaughter out there, I've com to realize how important family is.

Witnessing the unyielding love you have for your daughter, my granddaughter, Serosa, a love that drove you to the other side of the world, despite the unknown dangers that possibly could've awaited you, touched me in a way that most would not understand. Maybe, just maybe, if I had that same type of love and affection as a young boy, I could've been a better father to my son, Scorcher. You see, my lifestyle, the lifestyle of a drug czar, wouldn't let me let him leave the drug game for a better life. It was greed that drove me and power to instill fear in someone in order to control them. So when he told me of wanting to start a future with you, the only way I knew how to love him was through power."

Yasmina couldn't stop the tears from running down her face. As she listened to the words being read from the paper, the rage she felt made her want to strangle the messenger, for it was his tongue that spoke Shotty Dread's words. She continued listening.

"I know there's no way possible for me to right the wrongs of my life, nor change the outcome of how you feel about me, but I hope that by offering you fifty million dollars, it will help ease some of the pain I've caused."

The information was too much to handle. By the time the attorney finished reading, sweat beads had formed on Yasmina's forehead. There was something out of all of this that Yasmina now understood.

I now know why he abducted Serosa. She thought in silence. *If we met face to face, I was forced to hear his side of things.* Shaking her head, Yasmina thought, *Too bad things didn't turn out as he'd planned.*

After the finished he stood, shook hands with Serosa and Yasmina, and exited the room, leaving the policemen, to divulge their reasons for being there.

"Mrs. Love," one of the men acknowledged, "we only came to inform you that French authorities are not pressing any charges against you for what transpired at the Arc de Triomphe."

Yasmina's hear rate quickened then subsided as she exhaled a breath she was holding.

"But," the officer interjected, "although eyewitnesses, all with corroborated accounts and statements of what happened, said you were innocent of firing a weapon, we can't release you just yet."

Yasmina wrinkled her brow, "I think there are some spokespersons coming from the U.S. embassy to speak on your behalf . . . something about your charges in the U. S.; the escape from prison, and the death sentence, being pardoned."

The excitement of the news caused Yasmina, Serosa, Giddeon, and Brandon, to break into tears. They cried tears of joy. It wasn't until later that day, when the spokesperson informed them of Dalvin's heroic feat. It appears that he'd somehow gotten a recording of the President of the United States confessing to all sorts of crimes he'd taken part in while in the Senate. The crimes ranged from murder to extortion to bribery. The tape landed in the hands of someone working in the Pentagon, and an investigation was initiated. Unfortunately, when authorities arrived at the White House to arrest President Edgar L'Enfants III, they were saddened to find him slumped over in his chair, and a hole the size of a quarter just below his temple. He'd blown his brains out.

The ordeal was finally over. Yasmina learned about a side of Shotty Dread that she never knew and it made her sad, but not enough to shed anymore tears. S he couldn't hide the fact that he had stolen ten years of her life with the murders of her grandparents, Rosa, her best friend, Selena, and her husband, Scorcher. But, what was already done couldn't be undone and it was time to move forward.

"Who killed the gunmen?" she asked, eyeing Serosa, Brandon, and Giddeon.

There was silence. No one wanted to tell Yasmina that it was Shotty Dread who shoved her out of the way when the white gunman pointed a .9mm directly at her head and fired.

The first shot managed to catch her in the neck. If Shotty Dread hadn't reacted when he did, Yasmina would be dead.

The second shot, one fired from a .25 automatic, the same gun Yasmina held before being struck by the bullet, was fired by Shotty Dread. It caught the shooter dead center in the forehead. He died before hitting the ground, but not before his trigger finger involuntarily released a string of shots, one catching Shotty Dread in the chest, the other hitting him in the head. He died in his wheelchair.

Figuring to leave well enough alone, Yasmina said, "I'm just grateful to be alive." She caressed Serosa's head against her face.

In the passing months, Yasmina remained bedridden though her injuries had significantly healed. Prior to this day, she'd been back to the hospital to be operated on again, and now as she lay slightly groggily from the many medications she'd taken, she was awaken when hearing a noise.

Yasmina, yawned, moving to stretch as pain shot through her mutilated body. When the handle of the door flickered and a face jutted into view, Yasmina asked, "Damita, what was all that noise about?"

Damita ignored the question, smiling as she gently fluffed pillows placing them under Yasmina's back. She grabbed a remote and started pressing buttons until the bed elevated Yasmina almost into a sitting position. "I'll be back!" Damita exited the room, a smile still on her face.

In walks Giddeon dressed in a pair of beige slacks, a brown pair of soft leather Clarks, with a cream colored sweater. Tightly grasped in his hands was a bouquet of red roses. Leaning in, he kissed Yasmina and she smiled.

"I could bog you down all day with how much better you're looking, but I'm quite sure you're tired of hearing that." Pausing, he reached inside his pocket withdrawing a small box.

"I know we didn't start this journey together," he grabbed her by the hand, "but along the way, I've grown quite fond of you." With his free hand, Giddeon flipped open the small box and a yellow diamond came into view. "Yasmina, I fell in love with you the moment I laid eyes on you, and I know if we can make it through what we've been through in the past couple of months, we can survive each other for a lifetime." Looking deeply into Yasmina's eyes, Giddeon asked, "Will you marry me?"

Before Yasmina could respond, she was interrupted by a loud cry. Everyone's head abruptly turned. Yasmina was at a lost for words. Though she tried to speak, her voice wouldn't push out any sound. She could only watch as Brandon ushered Serosa inside the room in a wheelchair as she held close to her chest a feisty and wailing 71lb. 5oz. little girl.

"Momma," Serosa uttered, a tear sliding the length of her face. "After you give this man," she nodded in the direction of Giddeon, "his answer, you can hold your granddaughter, Destiny Oseira Love."

A wave of happiness consumed Yasmina, and for moments the only thing she could do was glance from Serosa, to Giddeon, and back to the others situated inside the room with smiles smeared across their faces.

Yasmina's hesitation to answer caused Damita to chime, "Girl, what's taking you so long. You know good men are hard to find these days, so when one comes knocking at your door, it's best you let him in before the neighbor beats you to the punch." Everyone laughed, but Yasmina's expression remained serious.

She looked at Giddeon, "I hardly know anything about you. I mean, what we shared when we were in Europe was extraordinary, I can't lie about that. And, as madly in love as I am with you, I don't know anything about you. What is it that you do for a living?"

Giddeon's facial expression changed. He looked sort of displaced. Eyeing Damita, he said, "I'm a stylist, I fix hair."

Damita's home was a joyous scene. For hours, Yasmina held her granddaughter rocking her to sleep while Serosa and Damita made up a list of the number of brides maids and groomsmen to be part of Yasmina and Giddeon's wedding.

Unbeknownst to anyone inside the house, danger was near. Two cars sat on each end of the cul de sac watching the house. The lady who watched over Serosa's newborn, Destiny, while she lived her first couple days in intensive care, was the same woman Yasmina had seen, both outside and inside, the Arc de Triomphe where the shooting began.

It won't be long before they all realized that it would be Destiny's burden to carry on a blood feud that'd started almost two decades before she was even born.

. . . The saga begins

AUTHOR'S NOTE

Hands down, this, out of four other novels that I have written and are waiting to be published, was the most difficult. The research was the most tedious process of all, which I'm grateful for the information given to me by people who reside in countries other than the United States.

Although I consider myself an urban – fiction artist, I don't limit myself by staying inside the box when I know there are other facets to the urban lifestyle. Many of them exist in countries abroad.

Please know that this story is told from my point of view, an urban-fiction art depicted about a young lady, Yasmina, who becomes estranged from her daughter, Serosa when incarceration separates them.

Their struggles to reunite, despite what society throws at them, result in a journey that most blacks in inner cities are faced with. How they overcome these obstacles shows the strength that African-Americans possess when faced with adversity.

Thank you for supporting my work.

Visit Shawn Black at www.realurbanlife.com and www.myspace.com/shawnblack/stick-n-move for comments and up and coming future projects.

Sample Chapters

From the book series

KWAME

By
Richard Jeanty

The Hero

The two men standing guard at the door didn't even see him coming. The loud thump of a punch to the throat of the six-foot-five-inch giant guarding the door with his life had the breath taken right out of him with that one punch. He stumbled to the ground without any hope of ever getting back up. His partner noticed the swift and effective delivery of the man's punch, and thought twice about approaching him. Running would be the smartest option at this time, but how cowardice would he look? The attacker was but five feet ten inches tall and perhaps one hundred and ninety pounds in weight. The security guard didn't have time on his side and before he could contemplate his next move, the attacker unloaded a kick to his groin that sent his six foot seven inch frame bowing in pain while holding his nuts for soothing comfort. Another blow to the temple followed and the man was out permanently.

At first glance, Kwame didn't stand a chance against the two giants guarding the front door. One weighed just a little less than three hundred and twenty five pounds, and the other looked like an NFL lineman at three hundred and sixty pounds. However, Kwame was a trained Navy Seal. He came home to find that the people closest to him were embroiled in a battle that threatened their livelihood daily. His sister, Candice, became a crackhead while his mother Aretha was a heroin addict. Two different types of drugs in one household, under one roof was enough to drive him crazy. Kwame didn't even recognize his sister at first. She had aged at least twice her real age and his mother was completely unrecognizable. He left her a strong woman when he joined the Navy eight years prior, but he came back to find his whole family had been under the control of drug dealers and the influence of drugs and Kwame set out to do something about it.

The two giants at the door was just the beginning of his battle to get to the low level dealers who controlled the streets where he grew up. As he made his way down the long dark corridor, he could see women with their breasts bare and fully naked, bagging the supplies of drugs for distribution throughout the community. Swift on his feet like a fast moving kitten, he was unnoticeable. He could hear the loud voices of men talking about their plans to rack up another half a million dollars from the neighborhood through their drug distribution by week's end. The strong smell of weed clouded the air as he approached the doorway to meet his nemesis. Without saying a word after setting foot in the room, he shot the first man who took noticed of him right in the head. Outnumbered six to one and magazine clips sitting on the tables by the dozen and loaded weapons at reach to every person in the room, Kwame had to act fast. It was a brief stand off before the first guy reached for his Nine Millimeter automatic weapon, and just like that he found himself engulfed in a battle with flying bullets from his chest all the way down to his toes. Pandemonium broke and everybody reached for their guns at once. As Kwame rolled around on his back on the floor with a Forty Four Magnum in each hand, all five men were shot once in the head and each fell dead to the floor before they had a chance to discharge their weapons.

The naked women ran for their lives as the barrage of gunshots sent them into frenzy. The masked gun man dressed in all black was irrelevant to them. It was time to get the hell out of dodge, to a safe place away from the crackhouse. Not worried too much about the innocent women, Kwame pulled out a laundry bag and started filling it with the stack of money on the table. By the time he was done, he had estimated at least a million dollars was confiscated for the good of the community. The back door was the quickest and safest exit without being noticed. After throwing the bag of money over a wall separating the crack house from the house next door, Kwame lit his match and threw it on the gasoline that he had poured before entering the house. The house was set ablaze and no evidence was left behind for the cops to build a case. It was one of the worse fires that Brownsville had seen in many years. No traces of human bones were *left, as everything burned town to ashes by the time the New York Fire Department responded.*

Kwame had been watching the house for weeks and he intended on getting rid of everything including the people behind the big drug operation that was destroying his community. Before going to the front of the house to get rid of the security guards, he had laid out his plan to burn down the house if he couldn't get passed them. A gallon of gasoline was poured in front of all the doors except the front one where the two securities stood guard. His plan was to start the fire in the back and quickly rush to the front to pour out more gasoline to block every possible exit way, but that was his last option. His first option was to grab some of the money to begin his plans for a recreational center for the neighborhood kids. His first option worked and it was on to the next crew.

When Kwame came home he vowed to work alone to get rid of the bad elements in his neighborhood. Mad that he had to leave home to escape the belly of the beast, Kwame came back with a vengeance. He wanted to give every little boy and little girl in his neighborhood a chance at survival and a future. He understood that the military did him some good, but he had to work twice as hard to even get considered for the elite Navy Seals. The military was something that he definitely didn't want any boys from his neighborhood to join. For him it was a last resort and in the end he made the best of it. Guerilla warfare was the most precious lesson he learned while in the military and it was those tactics that he planned on using to clean up his neighborhood.

A one man show meant that only he could be the cause to his own demise. There'd be no snitches to worry about, no outside help, no betrayal and most of all no deception from anybody. Self reliance was one of the training tactics he learned in the Navy and it was time for him to apply all that he learned to make his community all it could be.

Getting rid of that crack house was one of the first priorities of his mission. Kwame knew that the crack houses were sprouting all over the neighborhood and it would take precise planning on his part to get rid of them in a timely fashion without getting caught by the police. Kwame also knew that he wasn't just going to be fighting the drug dealers, but some of the crooked cops that are part of the criminal enterprise plaguing the hood.

The Man

A loner since middle school, Kwame was always intelligent and deviated from the norm at an early age. Nobody in his neighborhood dreamed about becoming a Navy Seal, but Kwame wasn't the average teenager. Considered a weirdo by most people as a kid for the way he dressed, he learned to be self-reliant by spending his spare time studying the martial arts. Kwame was one of the victims of a fatherless household. His mother, Janice, tried her best to raise her son to be a man, but Kwame would find his male role model at the dojo in his teacher, Kevin. He taught Kwame how to deal with his emotions, anger but most of all, he taught him discipline. Kwame was also a great student of the martial arts. He moved through the ranks in no time. By the time he reached sophomore year in high school, he had earned his black belt in karate.

Kwame tried his best to go through his daily life without any problems. He wanted to one day become a karate instructor to pass on the great teachings of his teacher Kevin. However, Kwame's patience would be tested by the high school thugs during his junior year in high school. No one knew of his martial arts training, but Kwame wore his sweats to school most of the time because it was easier for him to make it to practice everyday. While walking the halls on the way to his next class, Michael, the well-known thug of the school who practically robbed every student at the school of their lunch money at one time or another, confronted Kwame while his gang looked on.

"Hey weirdo, where's my lunch money for today?" he asked. Kwame kept walking and acted like he wasn't being addressed. Michael hurried to cut him off. "Didn't you hear me talking to you?" he shoved Kwame on his chest. "Look, I don't want any problems with you guys. I'm just trying to get to my next class," Kwame said. "Not before I get my lunch money for today," Michael reached to smack Kwame. Kwame's natural reflex caught Michael's hand before it could reach his face and with the strength of a bull, he started bending Michael's fingers until he begged for mercy in pain. Each time one of his goon tried to get closer to Kwame, he would press harder on Michael's finger forcing him to call off members of his crew. By the time Kwame let go of his hand, the assistant principal was making his way around the corner and screamed to them, "Get to class! The bell is about to ring!"

Like most bullies, Michael had a point to prove to his crew and a beat-down for Kwame was imminent. Armed with a twelve-inch knife and five flunkies to protect him in case he couldn't handle himself in a duel, Michael set out to even the score with Kwame after school. The embarrassment he suffered at the hands of Kwame earlier in the day was enough for his flunkies to question his leadership and heart. He needed to prove to them that he was a strong leader and that no one was going to get away with embarrassing him or anybody from his crew. Michael's reputation preceded him. He had never lost a fight to anyone at the high school and he wasn't going to allow Kwame the first W. Honestly, Michael had never had a fair fight in his life. A sucker-punch or completely blindsiding his opponent with a bottle across the face or a bat at the knees had been his ammo in the past. A fair fight to Michael was when he and his crew of almost ten guys beat another crew of two or three people.

Meanwhile, Kwame wasn't even thinking about Michael as he went about his day and hoping to make it to karate practice in time after school. Finally, the last bell rung and it was time to get out of school. Stuyvesant high had its history of troubled youths, but none had been as serious as Michael. As Kwame made his way down the block, Michael and his gang emerged and surrounded him. "What you gonna do now, chump?" Michael shoved Kwame on the chest again. Kwame spun around to assess his situation and his chances of victory against a gang of ten guys. The odds weren't in his favor, but his teacher also told him that odds didn't always matter, odds could also be changed. The element of surprise is always relevant and attacking an opponent or the enemy at the right time with the right combination of power can change those odds at any moment.

Like most chumps, Michael started talking loud to attract a crowd and within seconds a group of kids from the school gathered around to witness the next beat-down, courtesy of Michael. It was street cinema at its best, starring Michael and his gang, everyday after school at Stuyvesant high school. The only thing missing was the popcorn and comfortable seats. There had been many victims and none stood a chance against Michael and his gang. In this street saga, the bad guy always won. But things were about to change, a new star was about to be born and his name was Kwame. "What you gonna do now punk!" Michael yelled as he reached to shove Kwame in the face this time. However, like a scene in The Matrix, Kwame did a split to the ground and with his fist tighten, he forcefully delivered a blow to Michael's nuts and spun around like a breakdancer and kicked five of his cohorts in the knees simultaneously sending them falling face first to the ground. Each received a kick to the nuts and flinched in pain while the others made way for Kwame to walk away from the crowd unscathed.

Applauds could be heard from blocks as Kwame rushed home hoping that he bought himself enough time from those knuckleheads to make it home safely one more time. Kwame had changed the odds in his favor and he didn't even stick around for the glory that most kids would want to bask in. He was a simple man and a loner who had no fear and didn't allow people to push him around. The embarrassment Michael suffered in front of the whole school forced him and his gang to leave Stuyvesant high school and set up shop somewhere else at a high school in Manhattan.

The weird kid finally had a name and from that day on everybody referred to him as Kwame. He had gotten rid of a bully that had tormented students at the school for months. Even the teachers were afraid of Michael because he had slashed a few tires and broken a few windshields when he didn't get the kind of grades he felt he deserved without doing any work, whatsoever. It was good riddance and everybody could go back to learning again. The rest of his junior year went by without any problems.

Kwame was pretty much consumed by karate during his summer break. He would work his part-time job as a camp counselor at a local camp for kids in Brooklyn, and after work he would head straight to the dojo until closing. He worked relentlessly on developing new techniques that he could personally put to practice in case of emergencies. Kwame was even allowed to teach a beginner's self-defense class at the camp. And his students were very excited about his methodical approach to teaching. Kwame was often tested but never defeated. One night while riding the train home to Bedford Stuyvesant, a group of thugs tried to rob him of his paycheck. It was a Friday evening and most thugs understand clearly that it's payday for most kids who work a summer job. Not wanting to put in the work to earn their own keep, they were trying to get an easy score.

Kwame appeared to be the perfect victim. While at the booth trying to buy a token for the train, he pulled out the $150.00 that he had just gotten from cashing his check to look for a small bill to hand to the token clerk. He wasn't paying attention to the four thugs waiting in the wing, watching him, to make a victim out of him. After purchasing his token and making his way through the turnstile. The four thugs jumped the turnstile and began to follow him. He could feel the shadows lurking behind him like a suspenseful scene from a Bruce Lee action movie. The token clerk tried calling out the four bandits who didn't pay their way into the train station, but they vanished down to the platform. As Kwame stood waiting for the train, there wasn't another soul in sight. The four bandits split in a two groups of two's and after checking their surrounding and making sure that there were no witnesses or undercover police around, they decided to make their move.

With their knives in hands, two of them approached Kwame and demanded his money. "I don't have any money for you," he told them. "Listen chump, if you don't give up the dough, you're gonna end up in a body bag," said one of the thugs as he flinched his knife towards Kwame's stomach while the other one looked on. No other word was said as Kwame noticed the other two thugs a few feet away. It was a battle that was going to be determined by how quickly he could disarm the thugs one at a time. Kwame knew that he wouldn't stand a chance against four men armed with knives. So before the other two thugs could get any closer, he acted like he was going into his pocket to hand over the money. While one hand went into his pocket, the other hand went behind his back and a nunchukcs came out swinging, hitting the first dude closest to him right in the chin. The unanticipated blow knocked him down to the ground. A left kick met the other thug's lips and he fell back while the knife dropped out of his hand down on the train tracks. The other two thugs moved in swinging their knives like they were part of the cast of Westside Story, looking corny as hell. Kwame took notice of their inability to handle a knife. He set the first one up with a left hook, but as he stepped back to avoid contact,

Kwame's right foot found the other one's jaw. Down to the ground he went. Kwame was the hood version of Jean Claude Van Dam. He could kick an egg with his foot with exact accuracy. By then, one of the other thugs had gotten up and another one was still standing with a knife in hand. Swinging the nunchuck from right hand to left hand kept the two thugs at bay. Confusion set in and they had no idea how to defend against "The hood Bruce Lee." Kwame increased the speed of the nunchuck and fear started to take over the thugs. Bang! The end of the nunchuck hit the thug swinging the knife on top of his head. He's knocked unconscious and the other one takes off running. Kwame stood by and waited for the train to pull up. By the time he boarded the train, all three thugs were coming to and he simply flicked his finger like Dikembe Mutombo saying "no, no, no," and smiled as the train pulled away.

Kwame was a man of multi layers. Beside the martial arts, he was also a passionate artist who dedicated some of his time developing many comic strip heroes. He sort of lived through those heroes he created for his comic books. His imagination took him places where his main concern was always about making his neighborhood a safer and better place for all those who lived there. Robin Good was one of his favorite characters. Robin Good was a boy who basically robbed the drug dealers and gave the money to shelters and other organizations to help the poor. He had no special training except for his exceptional gift of gab and agility to get through small places. Robin Good could rob the president while charming the pants off him. He was very charismatic and knew how to turn on the charm to get even the most evil person to trust him. Kwame also developed a character named Mean Hakeem. Mean Hakeem was a character designed to fight injustice, police brutality and rogue cops. He was a well-trained martial artist with the military expertise to destroy a whole army by himself. Hakeem was also a motivator and a brave man. Hakeem believed in fighting for what's right and the betterment of his people in the hood. And his last character was Brainiac. Brainiac was a character developed to be a problem solver. He was a crime fighter who believed in using psychological approaches to solve crimes in the hood. Braniac could basically set up people and make them appear guilty even when they're not. His psychological tactics give him an edge because he can root out evil, liars and bad people very easily.

The first part of this book won't be out until fall 2011!!!

Sample Chapter

Hoodfellas II:
American Gangster
By
Richard Jeanty

Chapter 1

Haiti's clear skies, warm sunshine and inviting winds offer the perfect accommodating situation to explore the country's natural splendor. It's undiscovered, pristine trails, and foothills present the best opportunity for a serene bike ride. An abundance of outdoor opportunities reside in the back mountains of this precious island. The effervescent mood of the people is welcoming and embracing. With plenty of open spaces and green pasture for miles to come, warm climate and plenty of fresh Caribbean air, it's inexcusable to spend too much time indoor on this wonderful island. All of this aura brought a new sense of being to Deon Campbell. He felt rejuvenated when he first arrived in Haiti.

Deon thought he had left his criminal and troubled past behind and was hoping to start anew in a place where nobody knew his name. The fresh Caribbean air hit his face the minute he stepped off the cruise ship, and he just knew that the lifestyle of the rich and infamous was calling his name. With enough money to buy part of the island, Deon wouldn't have any financial worries until his calling from God. On the drive to Jean Paul's mansion caravan-style with a Toyota Sequoia ahead of him with armed security men and another Land Cruiser jeep filled with additional armed security men behind the limousine, Deon's mind was free to think about how he would miss his best friends and buddies, Short Dawg and No neck while riding in the air conditioned, long stretch limousine with his new friend, Jean Paul, and his entourage. He wanted to exact revenge on Short Dawg and No Neck's murderers and he would spend as much money it would take to make sure their killers don't live to see another day.

"I see you're a serious man and you're serious about your business," Deon said to Jean Paul as he sipped on a bottle of water while Jean Paul sipped on cognac. "In this country, you have to be. Don't let all the armed security intimidate you, it's a way of life here in Haiti," Jean Paul told him. An additional limousine also followed with all the luggage and money that Deon had to carry to Haiti with him. One of Deon's men rode with the second limousine driver. Keeping his eyes on the prize was very important and Deon didn't hide the fact that he wanted to know where his money was at all times. "I can't help but notice the worried look on your face, your money is fine. I have some of the best security men that Haiti has to offer…" and before the words could escape Jean Paul's mouth, gunfire erupted and bullets were flying everywhere from both sides of the road. A group of men emerged with machine guns as they attempted to stop the caravan so they could rob the crew. Deon had been in battle before, but this shit was ten times more than he had ever seen and he didn't know if Jean Paul had set him up or if they were just being robbed. "This fucking Haitian posse bullshit again!" Jean Paul screamed out loud. "Don't worry about a thing. All the cars are bullet proof down to the tires, but we're gonna teach these bastards a lesson, so they'll never fuck with me again. In each of those little compartments next to the button to lock your door is a nickel plated 9 millimeter, you guys are free to take out as many of them as possible. Their lives are worth shit here," he told them. At the push of a button, Jean Paul opened his compartment and pulled out two loaded .45 Lugar's. He cracked opened his window, and aimed at the pedestrian robbers. The crew of almost 20 men stood no chance as Jean Paul and his men returned fire with high powered guns from the barricaded bullet proof windows of the vehicles. A raid in Vietnam wouldn't even compare to the massacre that went on for about 2 minutes. After all the men were down, Jean Paul got out of the car to make sure that none of them had any breath left in them. It was like a firing squad as his men went around unloading bullets in the bodies lying across the pavement, ensuring that every one of the robbers was dead! The last crawling survivor received two bullets in each knee and one to the head before revealing that he was part of the Haitian posse located in the slums of Cite Soleil, the most dangerous slum in Port-Au-Prince, Haiti.

Even the United Nations guards, who are sent to monitor the situation in Haiti, were too afraid to go into Cite Soleil. The Haitian police feared confrontation in the slums because they were always outgunned and very few officers who went against the gang lived to tell about it another day. Jean Paul had been a target ever since his arrival in Haiti because he never hid his lavish lifestyle. A brash former drug dealer who grew up in the States, and was deported back to his homeland some twenty years later, he was not accustomed to the Haitian lifestyle or Haitian culture. After arriving in Haiti, Jean Paul had to learn his culture all over again. Americans like to say they're hungry enough to go do something drastic to feed their family, but in Haiti, those people literally lived it. Forced to eat dirt cookies due to lack of food, money and other resources, these gang members were tired of being hungry and anybody who got in their paths will pay the price for a better life, or better yet, food.

Many Haitian immigrants left Haiti with the hopes to one day go back to their homeland to help with the financial, economical, social infrastructure as well as democratic leadership. However, many of them usually find that what they left behind some twenty to thirty years ago has changed to the worst Haiti that they have ever seen. Since the departure of Baby Doc, Haiti has taken a turn for the worst and the economic climate in Haiti has forced many of its delinquents to become criminals of the worst kinds. While in the United States poor families are offered food stamps, subsidized housing and other economic relief by the government; in Haiti, relief only comes in the form of money sent to those who have relatives who live abroad. Those without relatives abroad suffer the worst kind of inhumane treatment, hunger, malnourishment, social inadequacies and the worst health.

To top off an already problematic situation, many of the Haitian politicians are unconscionable thieves who look to fill their pockets while the country is in dire need of every imaginable resource possible, including, but not limited to jobs, healthcare, social programs, education, clean water, deforestation, land development, any kind of industry and so on. Many of the elected officials offer promises, but rarely deliver on the promises after taking office. Most of the time, they become puppets of the United States government and in turn, look for their own self-interest instead of the interest of the people. Deon had no idea what he was stepping into and on the surface it appeared as if he would lead a peaceful life in the first Black republic of the world.

There's a price to be paid for freedom and winning a war against Napoleon's super French army with machetes and pure heart of warriors, the Haitians are definitely paying a pricc for it now. A brief history on the country was given to Deon and his crew by Jean Paul while on their three-hour drive to Jacmel from Port-Au-Prince where Jean Paul resided. Deon learned how Haiti, known back then as the pearl of the Antilles, has lost its luster and every resource it used to own due to deforestation. Coffee, sugarcane, cocoa and mangos are just a few of the natural resources and national products that the country used to offer the world, but most of it has evaporated because the government has not provided any assistance to the people to help them become self-sufficient in farming and land development. Security is one of the major reasons why foreign companies stay out of Haiti, and the government is not doing anything to bring back those companies as well as tourism, which helped the country thrive under the leadership of dirty old Papa Doc.

It was disheartening to Deon and his crew as they watched little kids running wild on the street digging through piles of trash looking for food along with the wild pigs and dogs on the side of the roads. Their faces reeked of pain, loneliness, hunger, starvation, malnutrition and hopelessness. Most of Deon's roughneck crew members were teary eyed as they watched this for almost two hours during the drive before hitting the scenic part of Haiti. Undeterred by the events that took place in the capital a few hours earlier, Deon ordered the driver to pull over in the center of St. Marc to hand out hundred dollar bills to a group of hungry children. The whole crew took part in handing out the money to the children who looked like they hadn't eaten a good meal since birth. Cindy took it especially hard as she was the only woman amongst the crew and Jean Paul didn't hide the fact that the minority two percent of white people in Haiti and another ten percent of mullatoes and people of mixed heritage controlled the wealth of Haiti.

It was evident who the wealthy people in Haiti were as they drove around in their frosty Range Rovers, Land Cruisers and other big name SUV's with their windows up as they navigate through the ghetto to rape the people of their wealth during the day while they rest their heads in their mansion in the Hills at night. The children rejoiced as Deon and the crew gave them enough money that would probably last them a whole month and more, to feed themselves and their families. Jean Paul was happy to see that his new friends sympathized with the people of Haiti, but he cautioned for them not to allow their kindness to